Tunnel Vision

Also by
Susan Shaw

One of the Survivors

Tunnel Vision

SUSAN SHAW

Margaret K. McElderry Books

NEW YORK LONDON TORONTO SYDNEY

MARGARET K. McELDERRY BOOKS

An imprint of Simon & Schuster Children's Publishing Division

1230 Avenue of the Americas, New York, New York 10020

MARGARET K. McELDERRY BOOKS is a trademark of Simon & Schuster, Inc.

For information about special discounts for bulk purchases, please contact Simon & Schuster Special Sales at 1-866-506-1949 or business@simonandschuster.com.

The Simon & Schuster Speakers Bureau can bring authors to your live event. For more information or to book an event, contact the Simon & Schuster Speakers Bureau at 1-866-248-3049 or visit our website at www.simonspeakers.com.

Book design by Mike Rosamilia

The text for this book is set in Adobe Garamond Pro.

Manufactured in the United States of America

10 9 8 7 6 5 4 3 2 1

Library of Congress Cataloging-in-Publication Data

Shaw, Susan, 1951–

Tunnel vision / Susan Shaw. — 1st ed.

p. cm.

Summary: After witnessing her mother's murder, sixteen-year-old high school student Liza Wellington and her father go into the witness protection program.

ISBN 978-1-4424-0839-5 (hardcover)

ISBN 978-1-4424-0841-8 (eBook)

[1. Witnesses—Protection—Fiction. 2. Organized crime—Fiction. 3. Crime—Fiction. 4. Murder—Fiction.] I. Title.

PZ7.S534343Tu 2011

[Fic]—dc22

2010036306

To
the girls,
the boys,
and Nancy!

Acknowledgments

Much gratitude to my editor, Alexandra Cooper, who came to me with the idea for *Tunnel Vision*. Many thanks also to all those who worked with her behind the scenes to help make this book the best it could be.

Also, thank-yous to John, Warren, Terry, and Martha for their kind and encouraging comments early on.

And one more thank-you to Alyssa Eisner Henkin, my agent, who is fantastic!

Tunnel Vision

Chapter 1

The laughing men weren't leaving much room for anyone to get by, but what else was I supposed to do? Stay in the underpass until Christmas?

The dim light silhouetted one of the men's Mickey Mouse ears. Not really Mickey Mouse ears, I told myself. Not possible. Or was it? I couldn't tell. But I had seen it was hat night at the place on the other side of the station.

"Excuse—"

ROARR! An express train passed overhead. Who could hear anything over that?

I glanced over the railing to street level, maybe five feet below my shoes, to where the lone car in the underpass bucked and stalled.

ROArrrrr . . .

Come on, guys. Out of my way!

The men were so loud, shouting and laughing. Mickey Mouse ears jumped with one of the roars and fell against one of his companions, a guy wearing a top hat. What a party!

"Charlie's had too much to drink," said the man closest to me. "Haw, haw, haw!"

The man was never going to know I was there, not with all that celebrating going on. *Maybe I should just go back and walk on the street,* I thought. No. This was the walkway, and these guys could just let me through.

I gritted my teeth and tried to find some sneaking-by room, maybe turn sideways against the railing and slip by like I was little, but there was just no space at all between that one guy and the railing. Zero.

The man's shirt creased against the rail as his laughter boomed out. "Poor Charlie! Haw, haw, haw!" Head thrown back, he laughed some more. "Haw, haw, haw, haaaww!"

I gave up and pushed the shoulder of the haw-hawer. "Excuse—"

He pivoted away from the group, and—*whoop!* I fell into the space that opened up as he did so. My grab for the railing brought the two of us nose to nose.

Garlic! *Whoa!*

I tried not to wince right in his face, so I grinned one of my goofy grins at him instead. Garlic Man frowned, but I just kept going, skirting past the now quiet, ominous-feeling group, its smoky shape undulating against my progress.

I kept saying it, "Excuse me, excuse me," like I didn't feel anything wrong or threatening, like I was just another perky girl on her way through, like everything was ordinary. "Excuse me, excuse me."

"Hey, girly-girl," said one of the men, and he reached out, curling and uncurling his fingers. I twisted my body to avoid his touch and pushed, pushed forward. I was afraid. The crowd opened for me, but not as fast as I wanted it to. I couldn't run, and I was afraid. "Hey, girly-girl!"

I pretended not to hear. "Excuse me, excuse me."

Then I was past them, and I *could* run.

"Hey!" That was Garlic Man. "Hey, girl! Stop!"

Stop? Stop? Uh-*uh*!

I fled out of the tunnel and into the dusky June air. Mom— yay, Mom!—stood at the next corner by our side yard, and I ran for her.

I ran for her, but I stumbled over an unevenness in the sidewalk and then another, dancing a couple of weird steps each time for the amusement of whoever was watching—Garlic Man or the Incredible Hulk or the guy with the fingers—anybody— before I could get my balance and keep going. Would I never reach her?

I was used to the old messed-up sidewalk, broken for ages, and I usually knew just where to put my feet without even thinking about it. Only, not this time. Somehow I couldn't time my steps right, not with that creeped-out feeling I still had. I kept tripping, the last time almost landing at Mom's feet.

Almost, because she caught me before I absolutely went down, her hands on my upper arms.

"Mom!" I felt like six instead of sixteen, just wanting my mom to make things right. I would hug her—I would tell her—and she'd—

"Li-ZA!" She jumped at me on the wavy "ZA!"

Bang!

We fell against the sticker bushes that lined our side yard, before hitting the ground.

"Ow!" What the heck? "Get off me!" Why did she do that?

Mom didn't move or answer, so I dug my elbows into the grass and pulled myself out from underneath inch by inch. "Come on, Mom, it's not funny." She was a dead weight on top of me. "Get off." She didn't move. Why was she doing this to me?

Inch, inch. What a time for a joke! Mom never played jokes like this. Why would she do it now? *Inch, inch.* And why wasn't she moving or laughing or anything? What was wrong with her?

"Come on, Mom!"

I gave a huge tug forward. Mom rolled off and over my right elbow, ending faceup on the sidewalk. Rolled and didn't move. Had she hit her head? I pushed to my knees and looked at her. She'd fainted, and that's why we'd gone down. That must have been it. She'd fainted and taken us both down.

But

Except

A red plume grew out of a spot just below Mom's left

shoulder. "Mom!" I didn't know much, but I knew to press against the plume. Wet and warm.

"What happened?" I asked her, but her eyes were closed. *Press, press!* "Why are you bleeding? One of the stickers get you?" *Pressssss!* "It must have been a big one."

Her eyelids fluttered. *Coming out of the faint,* I thought. She probably didn't even know about the sticker getting her. And all this blood coming out of the wound. It seemed like an awful lot for a sticker.

I heard the *Bang!* again, sort of in retrospect, and it started to register. Bang? Bang? There'd been a bang. But no one ever banged anything in our neighborhood.

Because, I guess, you just don't really believe anybody would actually, really shoot at your own mom. Maybe, anyway, I hadn't heard a *shot.* Maybe it had been a metal trash can lid hitting the sidewalk. But then wouldn't it have gone *clang?*

"Liza," Mom whispered. Her eyes darted up the street. "Danger." I looked around, but I didn't see anything except some kind of gray, unimportant fuss at the underpass. Unimportant to *me,* with trying to make Mom's blood stop running.

The street was empty, anyway, which was normal for this time of day, but we were on the sidewalk. Safe there from cars. What else was there to be safe from?

Then I snapped to some sort of reality. Mom was *hurt! Hurt!* "Somebody!" I shouted. "Help!"

There was noise all around me. That's what I was later told.

I don't remember it. It was all just Mom and the blood and the smell of the sidewalk in the sultry June air. A perfect June evening. How could this ever have happened?

But apparently two police officers had come out of a house near the underpass while I was with Mom.

They'd shouted, "Hey!" Something else I hadn't registered.

There'd been a scuffle, and the men I'd passed under the railroad tracks had scattered. So I was later told. One of the officers gave chase, and the other came down to me and knelt by my side. I remember none of that. Him, the noise. Nothing. What shooting?

Well, maybe all that was the unimportant gray confusion at the underpass. Everything was unimportant right then except Mom and how she kept bleeding. The blood was seeping onto the sidewalk behind her shoulder now. How could this be from a sticker bush?

"Help! Help!"

"It's on the way," somebody said, probably the officer, and I stopped shouting, just pressed and pressed, eyes only on Mom. She looked so pale.

Sirens. Ambulance. Noise. All in a jumble. I didn't know what any of it was, with my mind so much on Mom. The smell of blood, the salty smell of the sidewalk, Mom's dark red hair streaked against the white concrete, the dusky June air.

"Liza.

Liza.

Liza."

Dad's voice finally cut through, and I saw his face on the other side of Mom's chest.

I remember blinking and blinking at him. Somebody'd gotten him from our house, and he took over the pressing for me.

"Angela," he said to Mom. "Honey."

"Mmm," she responded, like it was just too hard. She turned her head, a crease between her eyebrows. "Danger. Liza. Guns."

Guns?

"No danger," said Dad. "Not now." And Mom's face seemed to relax a little, but not all the way.

I looked up the empty street. There'd been guns?

The *Bang!* replayed itself. Guns. Someone'd *shot* Mom? *Shot* her? *Mom?*

I pushed the hair away from her forehead. "You're gonna be all right," I told her. "Who shot you?"

"Liza," she murmured. "Little Liza Jane." From the folk song she used to sing to me.

"I'm sorry," I told her. "I didn't know why you pushed me down."

She smiled faintly. "My little flower." Eyes on Dad. "Harold."

Then the EMTs took her from us. Lifted her up and put her on a gurney and into the ambulance. There was a lot of blood on the sidewalk where she'd been. Or maybe a little blood looks like a lot. Maybe it wasn't so bad, I told myself. My hands were covered with red, and I wiped them off on my shorts before climbing into the ambulance, pulled there by an invisible rope that stretched, taut, between Mom and me. Wherever *she* was going, *I* was going. Dad came up beside me, and I noticed the red handprints on his white Phillies T-shirt.

"Not room for both of you," someone said, so we jumped out again and sprinted for the car. Just around the corner. Only around the corner.

"She's got to be all right," I hollered to Dad. "She was just standing there and—" *Woop-woop-woop!* The siren knocked out my words, and we ran harder. *Woop-woop! Woooooo!*

When we got to the Buick, I yanked on the door handle, but my fingers slipped off and the force of the yank spun me around. What? Blood. More blood. But I'd already wiped it off, hadn't I? I wiped it off on my shorts again, wiped the door handle with the hem of my shirt, and then I could open the door. Wasted seconds. *Come on!*

More seconds wasted while I buckled my seat belt and Dad turned on the ignition. Finally, finally, we left the driveway and took the car over Butler Avenue to a left on Lancaster, and then on to Bryn Mawr Hospital. We hit some traffic lights, and I couldn't stand it that we had to sit there, three cars back, five cars back, seven cars back, but we got to the hospital as fast as we could get there.

It turned out not to matter about the three cars, the five cars, or the seven cars. It didn't matter how fast we got there at all.

Mom
didn't
make it.

Chapter 2

A man met us as we entered the emergency room. A man in a tan sports jacket and a yellow tie. He could have been a music professor like Dad. A composer of musicals.

"Are you the Wellingtons?" he asked.

"Yes," Dad said, but I just walked on past. Who had time for this guy?

"Mom?" I looked around.

"I'm so sorry," said the man anyway, "but it's bad news."

"Mom? Mom?" I saw people sitting here and sitting there, some looking bored, some with their eyes closed, one woman holding her arm. *"Mom?"* I began to feel panicky. "Where's Mom?" I asked a random person at the drinking fountain. "Angela Wellington. Where is she?"

The random person shook her head, fading into one of the chairs. Why didn't she answer?

A touch on my elbow, and I looked up at Dad.

"I'm so sorry," said the man again. He was still at Dad's side. There was something about his face I just didn't like. Why wouldn't he go away? Take his "sorry" with him.

"Mom!" This time I shouted it.

"Are you listening, Liza?" Dad asked. "Mom didn't make it."

Well, that was dumb. So dumb it was ridiculous. Of course the ambulance had made it here. Who was this man in the tan sports jacket, anyway, that he could be talking like this to us? They shouldn't let crazy people like that in hospitals. They could scare you.

But I knew Mom was okay wherever she was. Of course. She was Mom. "You're saying the ambulance got lost? Right." I gave the sports jacket guy a dirty look. Ambulances did not get lost in the straight shot between Avon and Bryn Mawr.

"I mean," Dad said quietly, "she died. She died on the way. That's what he says. They did all they could."

"I'm sorry." Tan Jacket's voice was tight.

"Let me see her." I didn't listen, wouldn't listen, and I didn't hear anything else the tan jacket guy said, was saying, or would ever say. He was going to wreck everything, talking like that. And time mattered. Why weren't we just going to Mom? Why were we listening to anybody when she needed us? Why were we listening to *anybody*? *Time—mattered!* "Just let me see her."

Seeing Mom would make it better. I knew that. Anybody would have known that. My mother, the lady who ran up and down stairs like a maniac and who made four rhubarb pies for the school bake sale every fall and who laughed louder than anybody else I knew, she wouldn't die. She couldn't.

I'd go in and see her, and she'd smile at me. She'd *always* smile at *me*.

The man in the sports jacket told us, but I wouldn't believe him. I wouldn't even look at him. Who was he, anyway, that he could say something like that? Dad and I—we didn't listen. We paid no attention at all and went straight into the room where Mom was waiting for us. Someone pointed the way. I don't know who. Someone who had sense.

"Mom?"

The room was cool and so still.

But right then, it was like there was still a chance. The air told me somehow that things could go either way, depending on how carefully I walked the tightrope. *Mom's just thinking of something else, that's all, but she'll move in a second and smile at us.*

"Mom?" My voice was loud in that quiet space.

The air felt cold now, and it wouldn't talk to me.

No. I held my breath and pulled a little harder to the left. *Come on, Mom. Show 'em they're wrong.* Dad and I moved closer to the bed. The tan jacket man had to be wrong. There'd been a mistake. Because here was Mom's red hair and everything. They make mistakes in hospitals. I know it, and her hair can't look like that if she—

Boom!

The meteor struck and crushed me flat. Then gravity released its hold, and I floated out from underneath the meteor, soaring up to the moon, going high, high, high, so high that my head drifted away from my body, bobbing on the end of a long, stringlike neck. The moon wasn't real, I wasn't real, nothing was real, nothing except the enormous ticking of my watch.

Tick, tick, tick, *tick, TICK!*

My neck shrank my head back into the room, where everything came too sharply into focus. I screamed and backed into Dad. No words, just screams. He held me and held me while the noise left my mouth. I didn't seem to have any control over it.

"Okay," he said. "Okay." Over and over. "Okay." But his hands were trembling against my back. "Kayokayokay."

Then my legs lost themselves in the firmament. I had no legs. I had no arms. I had no head or face or body. I wasn't there.

Dad guided the me who wasn't there to a chair and sat me on it. He kept a hand on my shoulder, and he looked down at me.

"Liza?" Then louder. *"Liza?"*

The room kind of came together, which was when I knew that it had come apart, come apart and come together again, and Dad let go of me. He watched me for a lo-o-ng second before leaving me there to cross the room. He leaned over the bed to kiss Mom. I found the strength to follow and do the same. Then I saw Mom's shoulder. Her whole left side. Blood. Just blood.

"Oh, Mom. Ah, no, Mom."

Dad's hand held one of hers while I stroked her warm forehead. Warm. Still warm. I wanted to comfort her.

"It's all right," I told her, stroking, smoothing her warm skin, her warm hair, touching her eyebrows. "It'll be all right."

We stared at her, memorizing her face, memorizing the feel of her skin, the redness of her hair. What else could we do?

Afterward Dad took my hand in his, and we left the room. The professor man was still there, right outside the door, his brown eyes on us. I didn't care. Mom was dead. What else mattered?

"I want to go home," I said to Dad. "Just home. Home." Which meant I wanted to go home to Mom, put my arms around her, feel the warmth of her touch and her breath on my cheek. She would be there and alive to comfort me, not here, where some other reality was playing out. "Home," I said. "Home." All this other stuff wasn't true. It was a nightmare, and if I went home, I'd wake up from it. I kept walking for the exit. I could hardly see it for the waves of darkness, but I kept going.

Pressure on my hand slowed me down. "We have to talk to Detective Sawyer first." Dad's words were quiet.

"Who?"

Dad indicated the tan jacket guy, the professor guy, the guy who couldn't keep his stupid mouth shut. "He's from the police. He got here ahead of the ambulance in case Mom could tell him something, but she never said anything else after we left for the car."

"How do you know?"

"You weren't listening," he said. "It's all right. Your mind was somewhere else, and it's okay. But Detective Sawyer told me before we went in to see her." Dad's voice shook on his last words.

"All right." But I wouldn't pay attention. We'd go someplace, and Dad and this detective person would talk. Whatever. Then we'd go home. And do I-didn't-know-what. But at least we wouldn't be here in this place of death. Mom couldn't really be dead, anyway. She'd be home. How could I think that way after seeing her? But I did.

Dad and I followed Detective Sawyer into a room with a table and some chairs. The smell of coffee. Boxed doughnuts with pink sprinkles. Pink? We sat down, and I pushed the sprinkled doughnuts away so I couldn't see them over the edge of the box. Pink! On a day like today—pink? Whose idea in the history of the universe was *pink*?

"What can you tell me?" Gray sounds that swirled into the gray air.

"Liza? Liza?" Dad's voice swirled around me. "Liza?"

I blinked my eyes until the swirls lightened and I could see the room again. A single sob escaped my throat, and Dad handed me a bunch of napkins from somewhere. I took one, but it didn't do much good. The tears just rolled out of my eyes like a string of liquid pearls.

"What can you tell me?" the detective repeated.

Oh, yeah. Him.

I looked at Dad through a fog. He shrugged at me. "You're the one who was there," he said. "You walked past the men in the underpass, didn't you?"

I took that shrug and gave it to the detective. "I don't know anything." I wiped the tears off my chin. Maybe the tears were slowing. Yeah. Almost down to just sniffing. "Mom is dead. What else matters?" Sniff. Blot. Sniff. So I did know. For talking purposes.

"You can ID these people," he said. "Why did they shoot your mother?"

"One of the men in the underpass shot Mom?"

The detective nodded.

"Why'd he do that?"

"That's what I want you to tell me."

I shrugged again. "I don't know."

"Can you describe them?" Detective Sawyer asked. "The officers couldn't get a good look at them."

"I really only saw one." I didn't mention the grasping fingers I'd avoided. What good would that do? I drew on one of the napkins with the detective's pen. "Probably he doesn't look like that," I said. "The mole on his chin looks more like a heart than the way I drew it. And sort of like a chocolate smear, too." I wrote *Garlic Man* underneath. "He stank. Oh, yeah. And there was a guy that might have been wearing a Mickey Mouse hat— you know with the ears like that, but I didn't see his face."

Detective Sawyer took the paper from me and studied it, nodding his head. "You're a good artist," he said.

"Mm." Who cared?

"You know who this is?" he asked.

"No."

"I don't think you saw this man in the underpass," Detective Sawyer said. "It couldn't have been this man."

I looked at him. "Why not?"

"Yeah," said Dad. "Why not?" Detective Sawyer slid the paper across to Dad, who gave it a good glance. "Oh."

"Oh?" I repeated. "Oh? What's that mean?"

"You drew a picture of Robert Bramwell," said the detective. "Robert Bramwell isn't going around shooting people."

I turned my questioning gaze to Dad. "He's a famous philanthropist," he told me. "He has drug rehab places all over the country, and he's donated computers to lots of schools. He's giving a lecture at the high school tomorrow night. So say the posters in all the store windows."

"With his picture on them," added the detective with some emphasis.

"Oh." I still had never heard of him. "Does that mean he didn't stand in the underpass today?" But I guessed I'd seen the pictures. Oh, yeah, in almost every window between the train station and Lancaster Avenue while I'd walked Jackie to the bus stop. Kind of annoying I'd found it, in a hardly-paying-attention sort of way.

I'd seen his picture. I'd seen his picture all over the place, and my scrambled brain had put it on the face of the guy who'd said "Hey!" I wondered what Garlic Man really did look like.

"Okay," I said. "Apparently I didn't see him. So I guess I'm no help."

I thought Detective Sawyer would leave then and let Dad and me go home, but he stayed put.

"Listen," he said, and his face was severe. "Do you know what the two police officers saw when they came out of that house up the street from where your mom was shot?"

"Well," I said. "Someone shot Mom." Two officers coming out of a house? This was the first I'd heard of it. "I guess they wanted to make an arrest."

"No, but what they *saw*," said Detective Sawyer, "was two guns aimed at you. At *you*. Aiming just out of the darkness of the underpass." He paused. "*After* your mom was shot. You were between them and your mother, and these men were aiming at you. That's why the officers jumped them so quick. So they wouldn't shoot *you*. The officers didn't even see her."

"But . . . ," I began. "But I didn't do anything. Why shoot me?"

And I thought of the dumb silly smile I'd had on my face when I'd walked by. I was going to get shot for having a dumb silly smile?

"I only walked past them," I said. "I didn't see anything. Really. The guy with the mole, or the guy I thought was the guy with the mole, turned around as I went by and said, 'Hey!' One of the other guys made a grab at me, but I didn't see his face."

"Oh, Liza," said Dad.

"It was creepy," I answered him, "but he didn't touch me, and nothing else happened. I got out of there. That's it. Then they shot Mom." I paused, reliving and reliving the moment. "And she saw it. She saw it coming, and she threw herself on top of me." I told them about Mom shoving us into the bushes and me not understanding why. "She saved my life. Oh, Dad." I looked at him. "This was all my fault. It's all because of me."

"It wasn't your fault," he said.

"I tripped on the sidewalk a couple of times as I ran to her," I said. "I guess I wasn't a good target until I reached her. Oh, man!" If I hadn't tripped, maybe I'd be dead and she'd still be alive. Maybe. It should have been me.

Neither of the men said anything.

"But why were they aiming at *me*? I was just walking up Butler Avenue like I always do. Millions of people walk up Butler Avenue every day. Nobody shoots them. Ever."

"You saw something." The detective's voice was insistent. "You don't know what you saw, but you saw it."

I shook my head. "I don't know what to tell you."

He stood up. "Well, if either of you thinks of anything, call me. And lock your doors."

"That's it?" Dad stood up too, and I pushed up with him. I guessed we were leaving. "Lock our doors? That's all the help you can give us? My wife is dead, and someone tried to kill my daughter, and you say '*lock your doors*'? What kind of junk is that?" His voice dropped to an ominous tone. "Lock your doors!"

"We'll watch your house, Dr. Wellington," said Detective Sawyer, "but you can help with locking up and being careful. Call if anything at all strange happens."

"Plenty strange has already happened," said Dad, "and I think you should at least see where Robert Bramwell was when my wife was shot. Find the bullet and see if it matches anything with his name on it. If Liza said she saw him, she saw him. She doesn't make stuff up."

"Dad." I pulled on his arm, but he wasn't listening.

"Don't you think we should at least start there?" His voice was high again. "Maybe Bramwell shot my wife. Who knows? Maybe he's not such a great guy after all. Maybe he does go around shooting people. Maybe he has one of those manias where he thinks he's king of the world and can just act any way he wants. *Arrest him!*"

"Sure," said Detective Sawyer. "We'll talk to him. But don't get your hopes up."

"I won't," I said before Dad could answer. "Why would a philanthropist want to kill me?"

"We have to at least ask," Dad said. "It's somewhere to start."

But I knew that it was useless. Arrest a guy because I saw his picture? Come on.

We walked out to the parking lot with the detective. "I'm sorry," I said. "Maybe I'll still think of something." But I knew I wouldn't.

What I remember of the car ride home is all those headlights coming at us. Headlights and headlights and headlights while I cried. Then the car stopping in the driveway and nothing to do but leave it and go into a house where Mom would never again run down the steps. Never joke, never smile, never anything.

This couldn't be happening. Someone turned out the light, but the light would come on again, wouldn't it?

Mom was dead?

I didn't have a mother anymore?

How can Mom be dead? How can anybody's mom be dead?

I didn't believe it, even though I'd seen her, and Dad looked so gray.

The lentil soup aroma escaping the Crock-Pot in the kitchen embraced me on the living room couch as I cried and Dad slouched by my side. My mother had the soup going in there, so how could she be dead? How could she stir the soup if she was dead?

Oh, Mom!

Telephones, doorbells, and the sounds of the night washed over me while lights went on and off inside my head. Sometimes Dad was next to me, and sometimes he wasn't. I didn't know what he was doing when he wasn't beside me, but he always came back. Through it all, the steadiness of the soup aroma made a lie out of the truth. None of this was happening. It was all a lie. Every bit of it.

Chapter 3

Dad was standing at the living room window that night, just staring. He turned when he heard me on the steps.

"Can't sleep?"

"I'm afraid."

"Are you afraid a guy with a gun is going to find you? No one's outside, and the doors are locked. Windows and doors. Everything." He held the cordless out. "First sign of anything, I'm punching numbers, so don't you worry. Plus, the police are watching."

"It's not that," I said. "It's just—remember the man with the mole? Robert Bramwell? I know I didn't see him, but part of me still thinks I did, and every time I close my eyes, there he is. He has a gun, and he shoots it. Over and over. He shoots it and Mom falls on me." I started to cry again. "She falls every time. I can't make it stop."

"Come here."

I put my head on Dad's shoulder, and he held me as the tears fell. "I want Mom back," I sobbed.

"Me too." He let out a big breath. "Me too."

After a few minutes, feeling just as bad as before, I detached myself from Dad's arms and headed glumly for the steps. What could be done? Nothing. But Dad kept a hand over one of mine, and he came up behind me.

"I'll sit on the bed until you're asleep," he told me. "And if you don't go to sleep soon, we'll come downstairs again and have some warm milk or something. Okay? If we have to, we'll stay up all night."

Dad didn't sit on the bed much. He started on it, but then he was up, wandering around the room, picking up my books or my old stuffed animals, looking out the window. But he was there, and that was what counted. Even with my eyes closed, hearing him move around the room felt comforting. He was there.

I concentrated on Dad's footsteps to keep Robert Bramwell and his gun away. Then I was dreaming that I was concentrating on his footsteps. Then I was just dreaming.

I woke up the next morning to the smell of coffee, and I knew Dad was downstairs ahead of me. I didn't remember any dreams past the footsteps one, and my head felt heavy. I wished I didn't know why. I wished I could feel disoriented and not remember why I felt disoriented. But I remembered. And it wasn't long before Robert Bramwell and his gun came back.

Bang! Fall.

Susan Shaw

Bang! Fall.

Bang! Fall.

I got out of bed and pulled on some shorts and a T-shirt as fast as I could. Washed my face in cold water and ran down the steps for the kitchen, away, away, away from the replays.

Dad was sitting at the table in there, staring at a mug of coffee when I came in. Just looking at him made what was real take over. The *bangs* in my head quit, and Robert Bramwell's ghost disintegrated and fell away.

"Good morning, Liza," Dad said. "Want breakfast?"

"Not really." But I put some bread into the toaster anyway and took the apricot preserves from the fridge.

Dad nodded. "Good idea to eat," he said, although it looked like coffee was all he'd had so far. And not much of that, to judge by the fullness of the mug.

The phone began ringing again. And the doorbell. You'd just about sit down from one, and the other would start. People at the door brought casseroles or flowers. Some of them were friends of my parents, some of them were Dad's students, and some of them were deliverymen or women. Nobody much came through the front door, though—Dad and I didn't want any company right then—and once I took a sprawled-out position on the sofa, it was all just a blurry parade. Noise and flowers and Dad walking back and forth.

Every now and then Dad would say something to me like, "Four chicken casseroles," or "Mrs. Pomeroy brought over some cookies." And the dark haze I lived in would break up a little bit and life would particularize. I'd see Dad with some covered dish or other in his hands. I'd close my eyes, and when I opened them again, he wouldn't be there. Or he would be, but he wouldn't have that dish in his hands anymore. Maybe another one, or maybe his hands would be empty.

"Flowers from the people on Broadway," Dad said one of those times. He let the screen door close behind him. How did he get there? He'd been in the kitchen last I'd noticed, and here he was staring at me through a bunch of white blooms.

"Hm!" I tried to clear my head, dig myself into a spot of reality. "Broadway?"

"One of the *Hearts of Avon* cast members heard about Mom on the radio."

"Oh, Broadway! Weren't you supposed to go there this weekend?" I asked.

"Oh, yeah. Well, I guess I won't. If there's a problem with the music, they'll just have to tell me about it over the phone. Just not today."

At first I answered some of the phone calls, but then I stopped. They were all people calling who wanted to talk with Dad. Mostly I didn't even know them, and they were all asking the same thing. Had they heard right? Was Angela really dead? And what could they do?

Nothing. What could anybody do? What a question! Still, it was good that people asked it. People were asking it, and they cared.

"At least there's that," I said to Dad when the fifth chicken casserole turned up. "People care. Too bad we don't like chicken so much."

He nodded. "It means we aren't adrift and alone," he said. "It gives us a cushion for the fall. And we'll eat it. Don't worry. We'll eat it."

Why didn't I feel the cushion? Or would it have been worse without it? It was hard to believe anything could feel worse.

When I answered the door, sometimes I saw a police car pause at the curb, but how could the officers know if one of those casserole people was the bad guy or not?

Anyway, there was no bad guy, except the one in the dream who followed me all over the place. At least not one who would come to the house. Why shoot me? I was nobody.

The whole thing was a mistake. The guys with the guns knew that, and they were in east Texas or somewhere by now. Not in this part of Pennsylvania. Not in Pennsylvania at all. Probably not even on the East Coast. Hardly even on the earth.

No one would ever catch them, and they didn't care enough about me to try it again. It was a mistake they'd just forget about. Liza who?

"Hi." The foggy mishmash of air broke up at one point, and there was Jackie in front of me. Her face was so sorry.

"How'd you know?" I asked.

"I heard it on the radio. Shove over."

I moved over, and she sat on the couch next to me, put her right arm around my shoulders, took my left hand in hers. Who knew how comforting that would feel! "What can I do?" she asked.

"Talk to me," I said. "I keep wanting to scream, and if you talk to me, maybe I won't."

"What do you want me to talk about?"

"I don't care. Tell me what you had for breakfast. Tell me where your dog buried your brother's homework that time. Tell me how muddy the creek is where we used to wade across. I don't care."

"All right." She was quiet for a few seconds, and I could almost feel her thinking. "How about those three-pointers in the game against Norristown?" she asked. "Boy, no one could get near you."

I nodded.

"Melissa and all the girls—that's all they could talk about."

I nodded again. "That was a lot of fun."

"Fun! You were amazing! Jellyfish Carter said you practically turned into the neighborhood fountain when it was all over."

"Jellyfish said that?"

"Yeah. Boy, you got his attention. The most bubbly thing in the world, he said. It made him smile for a week."

"Jellyfish. Can you believe he finally asked me out? I didn't think he'd ever notice, and now we're going out next week."

"Some guys are just slow," she said. "It took my brother five years to get up the nerve to ask his wife out on a date."

"Seriously?"

"That's what he says. Next time don't wait if there's a guy

you like. What if Jellyfish was as slow as my brother? You could be married with great-grandchildren by the time some guys will speak up."

I laughed. Then I felt bad. I shouldn't have been laughing. Not with Mom—

Silence, and I began to get that feeling once more, like that guy was going to come after Mom and shoot her again. *Bang-fall! Bang-fall!*

I shuddered.

"The creek is really muddy." Jackie's words were hurried.

"How muddy?"

"As muddy as a chocolate pie, and once, my brother—"

Jackie broke off, and I looked up. Dad and some other man were standing in front of us.

"This is the undertaker," said Dad. "Mr. Golshin."

Oh. The undertaker.

Jackie stood up. "I have to go anyway. Mom made me promise not to stay long."

And before I could protest, she was at the door. "Call me later," she said, and left.

Then I had to turn around, and there was this undertaker. Who ever wants to see one of those?

Mr. Golshin picked up our family portrait from a shelf. "Nice-looking family." He glanced at me. "You have your mother's hair. What an unusual color. Almost real red."

I touched my head. "Yeah, well." At least I had that from my mother. Dad's height, Mom's hair. Goofy face from some laughing ancestor. If I hadn't had such a goofy face, maybe none of this would have happened.

Then we sat down, and I couldn't listen. Whatever. Just do it. Get it over with and get out of here. I would have hidden in my room, except for the phantom gunshots that were everywhere Dad wasn't.

How had this happened to us?

After Mr. Golshin left, I looked at Dad. "Can we just take a walk, maybe? You don't mind taking a walk with me, do you? I don't want to go by myself, but I want to be somewhere else. Just for a little bit."

"I don't know about a walk around here," said Dad. "We'll get in the car and drive to Valley Forge Park. How about that? I don't think anybody with a gun would look for us there. We'll go get Jackie, and she can come too."

So I called her. "We'll walk to the arch or go over to the river," I said to her, "and look at the water. Have lunch at one of the picnic tables. If you come, I'll feel more normal." I glanced at Mom's knitting where she'd left it on the coffee table. "I just don't want to be here right now. It's spooky."

"Sure, I'll come," she said, "of course. Want Melissa and Isabelle to come too? I'll call them."

"No, just you," I said. "I don't think I can handle that many voices. We'll pick you up in a few minutes."

Jackie said she'd be ready right away, and Dad and I threw some food into a bag before starting off for her house. We'd gotten as far as the front step when a police car rolled into the driveway.

"Everything okay here?" called the officer at the wheel.

"Everything's fine," answered Dad. Right. Fine. Peachy keen, as Mom would have said. "We're going out for a few hours."

"Okay. We'll still come around." The officer turned his head to ease the cruiser out onto the street. We watched the vehicle leave our neighborhood and pull back into traffic on Butler Avenue before disappearing.

"All right," I said. "Let's go."

"Hmmm," said Dad, his hand on the open front door. "Keys, food, drinks—"

"Come *on*!"

"I'm not—"

Riiing! The cordless in the living room.

Dad rolled his eyes at me.

"Let's *go*," I said. "Whoever it is can leave a message. Come on."

Riiiing!

"What if it's Jackie?"

"It's not."

Riiiiiing!

"Better to answer it." Dad glanced around before returning inside. "Come with me."

"I'll just stand here." It was a really quiet Saturday morning. Nobody was even using a lawn mower.

I could look through the screen door to where the phone was and keep my eye on Dad, and then I could stand it. Sort of. I didn't want to go back in where Mom wasn't, and besides, the police car had just been here. Anyway, nobody really wanted to kill me. The whole thing was a mistake from start to finish.

Riiiiing!

"I don't like it," Dad said from the carpet. "Come inside." He put the bag of food down and reached for the cordless.

"There's nobody out here," I told him. "I'm fine."

Dad spoke into the phone. "Hello? Oh, hello, Catherine." Pause. "Yes, I'm afraid so." He turned his back and paced three steps while I fingered a rosebush leaf and listened to his usual answers.

I didn't want to listen, but I had to be near Dad to keep the Bramwell ghost away. I had to stay near, but that didn't mean I had to be inside where my mother's knitting lay. I could see Dad all right from where I stood. Good enough.

"Thank you, thanks." He turned again, paced another three steps, and looked at me. "Come inside," he mouthed. He motioned with his arm.

I made a face. "Oh, okay."

Dad turned away again. "No. We're fine. . . . No, no—"

I let go of the leaf, put a hand on the screen door handle and pulled on it. I took a step. This was so dumb. I didn't want—

Glitter.

Sparkle.

Knife!

Clenched hand, hairy arm, and

KNIFE!

Then I could see nothing except the knife and the hand with the blackened fingernail. A viselike grip closing over my gut and yanking me backward, my desperate hold on the door handle losing, losing, *lost* to the slippery air.

I grabbed, I bit, but found nothing to grab or bite—nothing. But that knife, he couldn't bring it in, not yet, not the way I was flailing at it. Kicking and grabbing and biting and getting nothing, nothing, nothing. Then one good kick where I got him on the leg.

His grip tightened. Oh, my gut! Could he squeeze me in half?

"Uh-uh-*uh*!"

My arms lashed out against the moving target. Kick, kick, kick! How long could I last? The knife, the knife, *the knife*!

This way, that way, glinting in the sun. Close and closer. Closer—he's going for my neck! *"AAAAAAHH!"* I CAN'T SEE IT! *"AAAAAAAAAAA—"*

CUT!

Chapter 4

"Hey!"

My arm hit the ground hard. My lungs choked empty. That was when I saw the knifer's face. A gold front tooth glinted in the sun, and a big lump stuck out on the side of his forehead. *Blink.* Gone!

Dad tore past, then raced over lawns behind the man, toward the woods at the end of the street.

If Dad caught him, if Dad caught him—*the knife! Don't catch him!*

It hurt to breathe. "Dad! Come back! Dad!" The words barely squeaked out. No way Dad could hear them.

I watched, so helpless. Dad ran faster than I'd ever seen him, his long strides narrowing and narrowing the distance to the knifer. Metallic flashes from the man's right hand punctuated the air.

Don't you see the knife?

My neck stung where the knife had sliced me. My arm hurt too, and so did my chest. I tried again to yell, but coughed instead. The thug got farther and farther away from Dad, then disappeared into the woods.

Dad gave up. He turned around and came back, panting.

"He was too fast." I noticed Dad still held the cordless in his left hand. "Oh, my God! You're cut!" He dropped beside me. "Good God!" He put the phone down and reached into his pocket for a handkerchief. "Does it hurt bad?" He put the handkerchief against my throat, and I held it there. "I was only in the house for a minute. And the police officer had just been here." He glanced around. "Where is he now?"

I took the cloth away from my neck and looked at it. Red, but not too much. I'd been lucky. "He just nicked me," I rasped, "thanks to you." I pressed the handkerchief on my neck again, thinking about how I'd pressed against Mom's shoulder, trying not to think about Mom and what had happened to her.

"He could have killed you," said Dad.

I tried to clear my throat. "I'm glad he got away. He could have killed you, too." I closed my eyes. Adrenaline raced, raced, raced through my body. I felt sick to my stomach, and my throat hurt so much from all the screaming, I hardly noticed the cut on my neck.

"Does it hurt bad?"

"Not so much." I opened my eyes. "What in the world is going on around here?"

Before Dad could answer, a shadow threw itself across his face, and I looked up. Neighbors circled around us—talking, talking, talking—wanting to know what was wrong. I never heard them at all until I saw the shadow.

Mrs. Pomeroy held a broom. "Are you okay, honey?" she asked.

"Why'd ya scream?" asked Jellyfish. Oh, man, did he have to see me like this? "Hey, you're bleeding." He had a paint-brush full of blue paint in his hand. He was covered in the same blue.

"What's going on?" asked Mr. Solomon. "I saw you chasing that man in a golf shirt, Hal. What did he do?"

Jellyfish's mom and dad came up too. Everybody's eyes widened to the size of old-fashioned dollar coins when Dad and I told them what had happened, and I just wanted to hug all of them for caring so much, even Jellyfish, house paint and all.

I pointed at him. "What happened to you?" I asked.

"I knocked the bucket over from the stepladder when you screamed," he answered.

"The color suits you," said Dad.

And even with the scare, that made everyone laugh. I looked at Dad. He made a joke? Mom's dead, and he made a joke? He wasn't smiling, though.

"Sorry," he said to me. "I'm on automatic, I guess."

"It's all right," I said. "Doesn't matter."

How could it matter?

Dad helped me into the house and onto the couch while

everybody else followed. Jellyfish called the police from his cell phone. The paintbrush wasn't in his hand anymore, and I kind of wondered where it had gone.

"I left it in the grass," he explained without my even asking him. How'd he know what I was thinking?

His mom brought me a glass of water from the kitchen and dabbed my neck with a damp towel. Such a gentle touch.

"Not too bad," she said. "Not too bad." She put a bandage over the cut, and I thought how well she knew us to know where we kept the bandages in the kitchen. I loved her for knowing. I loved everybody in the room.

"This is terrible," Dad said. "Who would hurt Liza? Who would hurt Angela? This is terrible. Terrible. Terrible, terrible, terrible, terrible." He paced back and forth as he spoke, his voice dropping with each utterance. Mrs. Pomeroy put her arm across his back and paced with him, broom and all. "Terrible." The word became a whisper while the two of them paced. I watched the other neighbors' eyes follow them from one side of the room to the other. Eyes in sad, serious faces.

The doorbell rang. Dad and Mrs. Pomeroy came to a rest by the sofa while Jellyfish answered the bell. In came Detective Sawyer. I didn't move at all, just lay there while everybody else talked.

"You saw the man?" he asked.

"I didn't see his face," said Dad.

"I did." My breath was coming back, and my chest didn't feel quite so awful.

Detective Sawyer took a seat opposite from me and opened his laptop on the coffee table next to Mom's knitting. He pushed the knitting a little to the side to make enough room, and I hated that. Mom had left it there.

Don't touch it. Don't anybody ever touch it. Leave it the way it all was before any of this happened. If you don't, how can Mom come back?

"What did he look like?" Detective Sawyer asked.

"He had a gold front tooth and a lump the size of a golf ball on the side of his forehead." I considered. "Right side. He was white. Maybe six foot. Could have had blond hair, but I think he was mostly bald. With a blond fringe. He was also fast. And he had a knife."

"Your mind is like a camera," said Mrs. Pomeroy.

"I couldn't catch him," said Dad. "He was fast."

"Well, he had a knife," I reminded him. "You didn't want to catch him. Not really."

"He was a couple inches shorter than you, Liza," said Jellyfish, "if he wasn't taller than six foot." And maybe that was the reason I could fight with the guy long enough for Dad to notice and shout "Hey!" Long enough to not get really cut with that knife before the creep dropped me.

Detective Sawyer punched a few keys on his keyboard. "Do you see the man?" He aimed the screen at me and showed me, one after the other, a bunch of pictures.

"No. No. No. No. Oh, that's him."

"You're sure."

"Yes." And I was, except that the picture didn't show the lump on his head. I told Detective Sawyer that.

"Mm. It could have grown since the picture was taken. His name's Gary Carmichael. Do you know him?"

"I've never heard of him."

"Well, there has to be a reason he went for you."

I couldn't answer—just shook my head. Shook it and shook it.

Then everything went sideways and wrong. The air turned blue and thick, and the coffee table warped from a rectangle to a diamond. How could those corners pull and push like that?

I almost laughed, except it was so horrible. Sounds were wrong, sights were wrong, the air was wrong.

I gasped and gasped in the wrong air. Not laughing, not crying, just trying to get oxygen from that thick blueness. What was I doing? I blinked at Mr. Solomon and caught him with his lips pursed into a perfect *O*.

"Steady," said Jellyfish through the swimming air. He handed me the glass of water I'd left on the table. I tried to drink it, but my hand shook so much, the water went over my fingers, shocking the blue away with its coldness. Jellyfish put his hand over mine and stopped the shaking so I could drink. Two swallows. It's all I could choke down.

"Okay." I blinked a couple of times. "Okay." And Jellyfish helped me put the glass back on the table. A little piece of me thought of Mom and "Coaster, Liza!" But I couldn't do anything but see the wet glass against the wood. Cold wet glass. "Coaster, Liza!"

The detective tapped the coffee table with an index finger. "This is the second attack," he said. "Someone killed your mother last evening, but that person was trying to kill you, and now *this* man tried to kill you today. Did you see him in the underpass yesterday?"

"No."

"Are you sure?"

"I don't think I'd forget that face."

I leaned forward and moved the glass to a coaster. *Sorry, Mom.* Still water on the table, though. I brushed it into tiny beads with the palm of my hand. *Sorry.* I took the wetness and rubbed it onto my cheeks, trying to lose the *Twilight Zone* air. Better. A little.

"What about the other guy?" Dad asked. "Robert Bramwell? Did you question him? Did you find the bullet?"

"Robert *Bramwell*!" The neighbors' voices chorused together unevenly.

"He's not our man," said Detective Sawyer. "Bramwell was in Atlantic City last night. With a whole crowd of other people. And we have not found the bullet, no."

"I got it wrong." I looked at Jellyfish. "The guy who shot Mom looked like Robert Bramwell to me. But I guess I was just confused."

"Nobody looks like Robert Bramwell except Robert Bramwell," said Mrs. Pomeroy. "The ugliest man in the entire universe.

Good thing for him he's rich. That's some compensation for him, at least." She paused. "You think he shot your mother?" Her voice was incredulous. "Mr. Good Guy?"

"No," I said. "I don't know who did."

"But you're sure it wasn't Carmichael." Detective Sawyer made it a statement.

"Well, I didn't see him," I said, "but I didn't see anybody do the shooting. I have no idea who was in the underpass."

He rose. "I need to call this in. Maybe we can catch this Carmichael fella before he gets too far. This might be the end of the line for him."

The detective went outside, and we could hear him speaking into his phone from the front walk.

"Why did he go outside?" I asked. "What's the secret?"

But before anyone could answer, our telephone rang. Dad answered the cordless that was again in his hand. "For you," he said. "Jackie."

"Oh! Jackie!" I took the phone into the kitchen, stopping on the way for a two-second hug from Jellyfish. His shoulder against my cheek felt so good!

Then I left him and all the other serious-looking people in the living room and brought Jackie up to date. I told her I didn't think we were going to the park after all.

"Then I'll come over," she said.

"I don't know," I said to her. "I don't think we're finished with the police yet. I'll call you later."

I returned to the living room. The neighbors had left, and

Dad and the detective stood together by the door, apparently waiting for me.

"We're going downtown," Dad said. His laptop case hung by its strap over his shoulder.

"What? Why?"

"Somehow," he told me, "this is now an FBI matter."

Chapter 5

A police officer named Larry took Dad and me to a huge building in Center City Philadelphia that looked like nothing but windows from the outside. Somehow I'd always thought that FBI offices wouldn't be so much right out in the open, would maybe be down some back alley behind an ivy-covered door or a place you could get to only through the kitchen of a Chinese restaurant, and needing a password on top of that.

Nope. Big and bright and in your face. And a sign: WILLIAM J. GREEN BUILDING. Well, maybe that was the secret part. Who was William J. Green? Someone like Robert Bramwell?

Larry parked the cruiser and took us to the building. What a windy day! My hair flew all over the place so I could hardly see where I was going until I clamped it down with both hands.

Thinking of the two ponytail holders on my bureau at home did me no good at all.

We went inside and took an elevator up to the eighth floor, where Larry spoke to a lady in a blue jacket, an ID badge fastened to her pocket. She smiled at us over Larry's shoulder and directed us to a room down the hall.

"The agents will be with you shortly," she said.

"Agents?" I asked Dad, but that was when Larry opened the door for us. We entered a room that contained a scattering of tables and chairs. A window showed us a view of the building across the street.

"Good luck," said Larry.

"Thanks," said Dad. "We appreciate it."

The door squeaked closed behind him, and then it was just Dad and me in a room so quiet all I could hear was the hum of the overhead lights.

I went to the window and looked down. A long way down. Two fire engines went by, lights flashing, their sirens cutting through the silence of the room.

"Why do we have to be here?" It was a variation on the questions I'd asked all the way from home: Why do we have to go? Why couldn't we stay home? How come we couldn't go to the park? "How are we going to get home if Larry drives back without us?"

"If Larry has to leave, someone else will take us back." Dad's grin was ghostly, but it was a grin, the first I'd seen on his face since I'd left to take Jackie to the bus the previous evening. Was that only the day before? "I'm pretty sure they won't push us out into the street and make us walk home."

"But why are we here?" for the millionth time.

"I told you." He put his laptop down on one of the tables.

"Why'd ya bring that, anyway?"

"That was Detective Sawyer's idea. It has all my contact information in it. And my schedule. Why someone might want to know that, I'm not sure, but it's handy for them."

"Well, anyway, coming here doesn't make sense." I paced back and forth while I spoke. "We stumbled into an FBI case, and they think we know something useful. We don't. Why can't they just believe us and leave us alone? We're not really part of this. It was a mistake."

I unslung my purse from my shoulder. I wouldn't have brought it except for the last minute suggestion from Detective Sawyer: "Grab your purse." Nothing useful in it except my wallet, and nothing useful in *that* except my learner's permit. Not even a brush, which wouldn't have been a bad thing to have right about now.

I dropped the purse by the laptop and looked at Dad. Had he even combed his hair today? "I wish we hadn't come."

"Don't you want to help find who killed Mom?"

"Sure. But I don't know anything, and I don't like it here."

"Maybe if they ask the right questions, you'll think of something. Or I will."

"I doubt it. Let's go home and let them wonder where we are. The train station's around here somewhere, isn't it?" Then

I thought of the underpass next to the train station on Butler Avenue, and I was sorry I'd said that.

"Liza. Come on. Maybe this will help Mom somehow."

I shrugged at him before again staring out the window. Endless, endless traffic streamed below. *Nothing can help Mom.* I didn't say that out loud, though. Still, I wondered how doing anything at all could help her.

A blue car made a left turn and then disappeared. Then a green one. Then another blue one. Where was everybody going? And why'd they like blue cars to do it in? What was so important? A motorcycle came to a stop just below, and a leather-jacketed man got off it. I concentrated on following his progress across the street, even though he kept disappearing around buses and cars. Where is he now? Now? There he is. There. There, now. There. There he is.

The door behind me squeaked open—probably Larry again. Maybe he wasn't leaving us here after all. Maybe he'd just gone out for coffee—but I still followed the motorcyclist with my eyes. Where was he going?

"Dr. Wellington? Liza?" Not Larry's voice.

Dad pulled me from the window, and faced me the other way. Not Larry at all.

"I'm Kevin Oberman." He was a tall man with pale cheeks colored with uneven pink. Like he'd been running. He indicated the woman beside him. "Rebecca Harris." She was short and blond with dark red lipstick. Also, she had a yellow-ribboned teddy bear under her arm. "We're FBI agents."

Had she been on her way to a kids' party? Was there a cake with candles in the next room? Or was the party supposed to be in here after we left? I looked around. It didn't seem like a very good place for a party.

Dad shook hands with the agents, and then I did too.

"We're sorry for your loss," said Mr. Oberman.

"Thanks," said Dad, but I didn't say anything. Maybe we'd leave faster that way. Get away from this place with the sirens sneaking in past the quiet.

"Please." Ms. Harris gestured with her free hand toward the sofa nearest the table where Dad's laptop and my purse lay.

Dad and I took that sofa, and the agents each took a chair on the other side of the table.

Ms. Harris handed me the stuffed bear. "I know you're too big for this," she said. "I'd understood you were about five. It's yours, though, if you want it."

"I'm sixteen," I said. Maybe I was too old for it, but I took the stuffed bear and hugged him anyway. He smelled of foam. "Thank you." Ms. Harris gave me a brisk nod, her eyebrows drawn high.

"So," said Dad, "you wanted us here?"

"Yes," said Ms. Harris, "and we thank you for coming." She looked at her partner.

"To get to the point," said Mr. Oberman, "we understand that Liza was attacked by Gary Carmichael this morning."

"He grabbed me and cut my neck with his knife," I said. "I'm okay, though."

"Good," said Ms. Harris. "Are you sure?"

I touched the bandage. "It was just a nick."

"And you know it was Gary Carmichael who did it?" asked Mr. Oberman.

"I identified his picture."

Mr. Oberman took a photograph out of a file folder and held it up. It was a group shot, a bunch of men on a pier laughing and holding fishing poles. "One of these guys?"

"Different picture but same guy," I said. "Third from the left. He's the one." But— "Wait." Somebody else in the snapshot caught my eye. I took the photograph and squinted at it. Yeah. The guy from the underpass with the Mickey Mouse ears. That was him. I must have seen more than his silhouette if I remembered that scar beside his mouth. I turned the picture so the agents could see it, and I tapped the image of Mickey Mouse Man with the knuckle of my index finger. "He was in the underpass. I think his name is Charlie."

"Charles McVoy," said Ms. Harris. "We'll look for him."

"I didn't see him do anything wrong." I remembered him falling against another man during all the laughter. Drunk. Whatever. "I just saw him."

"Recognize anybody else?" asked Dad.

I studied the picture again. "No."

I gave it back to Mr. Oberman, and he put it away. "So you recognize Gary Carmichael as the person who attacked you?"

"Yes."

"Would you testify in court to that effect?"

To that effect? Was that how people really talked? *To that effect?* Were we on television? *To that effect?*

"Oh," said Dad. "You've caught him?"

I let out a huge breath. *Haahh!* "That's the best news I've heard all day." I stood up. "Let's go, Dad. Case closed."

"It would be good news," said Mr. Oberman, "if we had caught him. He's still out there."

"Ohh." I slouched back into my seat. "What's the point, then?" I asked. "How can I testify against him if you don't even know where he is?"

"We'll catch him," said Ms. Harris, "eventually. So you'll testify? So that when we get him, we can keep him off the street?"

"Fine," I said. "Can we go now?" Dad's hand on my arm pulled me back down as I again started to rise.

"I don't like where this is heading, Liza," he said. "It could be dangerous."

"It sure could be," said Ms. Harris. "We should discuss it a bit longer before you decide. It'll be up to both of you."

So they asked me some questions about Carmichael and his knife and about what happened to Mom the night before. I wasn't sure why that part mattered to them, because I couldn't tell them anything worthwhile. All I knew was that Mom was dead, and talking about it made me cry.

"Here." Ms. Harris grabbed a box of tissues from another table and handed it to me. "I'm sorry, but we have to ask these questions."

"I don't know why." I dabbed my eyes. "But okay." And we kept going.

After what seemed like forever, Mr. Oberman said, "All right. That's enough for now."

And then the room got quiet again while all my answers sank through the chairs and the sofas and the carpets like five-hundred-pound weights. Mom was dead. That's what it all seemed to say. No more, no more, no more.

I sighed and picked up my bag. "Well?" I looked at Dad.

"So you'll testify?" asked Ms. Harris.

"Sure, I guess."

"No," said Dad. "She doesn't need to keep living through that."

The agents glanced at each other before looking back at us.

"Well, here's something you need to understand," said Mr. Oberman. He cleared his throat. "Whether Liza testifies or not, her life is in danger. Your life is in danger too. You didn't see Carmichael's face, Dr. Wellington, but he doesn't know that." He went on, telling us all about Gary Carmichael. Violent, but never convicted. Rarely caught.

"Even if he wasn't on the loose, even if we caught him this minute," added Ms. Harris, "you'd still be in danger. Carmichael's part of a huge gang. They call themselves the Core. The one time we caught Carmichael, we had to set him free after our only witness was killed. We're certain the Core was behind it, but we didn't know enough to arrest anybody. That could happen again."

I swallowed. It could happen again? With me as the witness

it could happen to? The one who would end up dead? What had I ever done to anybody? Shoot baskets?

"But," I said, "isn't there some way to stop them? I didn't do anything. Can't you explain—"

"Oh, my God!" Dad leaped to his feet. "You want to *relocate* us! That's why we're here. Who do you think we are? The Mafia?"

I stared at Dad. *"What?"* I stood up beside him, and the teddy bear fell to the floor. "Mafia? Huh?"

"We think," said Ms. Harris, and her voice was soft, "that you are a couple of good people who won't live very long if we don't act quickly."

Pause.

Dad and I stared at each other.

Pause.

We stared some more. I was shaking my head. *No. No. No.*

"You want us to leave now?" Dad's voice was quieter. He wasn't looking at me. He was looking back and forth between the agents.

"Now?" I repeated. "Now? As in—*now?*"

"That's right," said Ms. Harris. "You won't be able to go home again. You shouldn't." *I'm sorry for you*—that was what her face told us.

"That's why," Dad said. "That's why, isn't it, I was told to bring my computer, because Detective Sawyer thought I wouldn't be coming back for it. Because I told him I have research for a book in it. And it might get lost."

"And my purse," I said, looking down at the almost useless thing. "He told me to bring it." I could picture my cell phone sitting next to the ponytail holders on my bureau. Wished I'd brought that.

"You might want those things faster than we can bring them to you," said Ms. Harris. "Plus, sometimes computers do get damaged. Purses disappear."

I shook my head. "No. You can't keep us from going home." What about Jellyfish? What about Jackie? And my other friends? What about school? "It's home. Everybody can always go home."

"We can't guarantee your safety if you go home," said Ms. Harris. "We could almost guarantee you . . . something else." She paused before the last two words. They came out a little slower than the ones preceding them.

I ran my fingers over my face and through my hair. "How did I get mixed up with these people?"

"It doesn't matter," said Dad. "We have to deal with it."

"I'm just a basketball player," I said to the agents. "I—I shoot baskets. My team won states this year. Could that be what this is about? Somebody doesn't like it that we won states and that I got the most points?" I wished I could give them back, give back all the basketball games I ever played, trade them all for a rewind of the last two days.

Mr. Oberman shook his head. "I really don't think Gary Carmichael attempted to kill you because of your basketball skill. He has a bigger history with things like drugs and money laundering. And murder."

"Well, I have nothing to do with those things. I do homework and play basketball." I looked at Dad. "What else do I do? There must be something else I do."

He didn't answer.

"We'll look into the basketball angle," said Ms. Harris. "We have known of such things. But it's unlikely."

Then everybody stopped talking. Mr. Oberman got up and stretched. Ms. Harris stood and paced the room while checking her cell phone for messages. Dad and I—we didn't move. Just stood there between our former and future lives. Somehow, where we stood was the borderline. In a minute, I knew, we were going to have to do something besides stand there. We'd have to move forward, crossing the border into a life I didn't want. *Freeze this moment!* What would we do?

"So." Ms. Harris paused behind her chair and let the word hang. She reached over and picked up the teddy bear, rested it on the sofa behind my right leg. "Will you testify, Liza? Will you let her testify, Dr. Wellington?"

I looked at Dad.

"I don't like it," he said. "It puts Liza at an awful risk."

"It will put your wife's murderer away." Mr. Oberman's voice was soft.

"I don't care." Dad's voice wasn't soft. "I'm not losing a wife *and* a daughter."

I sighed. "All right, Dad. Let's go. It's over." I reached for my purse. My almost empty purse.

"We can't protect you if you don't agree." Mr. Oberman

spoke quickly. "That's the way it works. It's up to you, of course. We can't make you. But you'll be unprotected."

"It's too dangerous," Dad said. "Think if it was your daughter."

I moved my eyes to the agents, first Mr. Oberman, then Ms. Harris. They were looking at each other, not us, like there was something they knew but weren't saying. Not out loud. But I got it.

"I'll live ten minutes," I said to them, "won't I, if I go home? Ten minutes."

Mr. Oberman's gaze dropped to the floor, but Ms. Harris looked straight at me.

"Maybe that long."

I felt my eyes widen. *"Dad!"* Make this not so!

"These are dangerous men," said Mr. Oberman. "And women. They don't play games. They aren't softhearted and don't have good sides. They will kill you."

"But—" I locked eyes with my father. "Dad!"

"We have to relocate, Liza. You know we do."

"Oh, Dad, I don't want to. Please?"

"We have to do it," he said. "You'll have a future."

"But," I said, "we didn't have Mom's funeral yet."

"I know."

"And I'm supposed to go to the movies with Jellyfish next week. He finally asked me. *Jellyfish!"*

"I know."

"And school's not over. I have another three days before

finals. I can't miss finals. And that last report for English is due Monday. My last . . . re . . . por . . ."

Dad didn't answer this time, and the others just waited while my sentence wilted onto the rug and died there.

Leave? Just leave? Not see anybody I knew ever again? Jackie? Kyle? Jellyfish? My friends. My pizza-loving friends. How could I leave my *friends*?

I felt like soggy cardboard. The light was wrong, and everything had a funny sound. Chairs scraped dryly on the carpet, people cleared their throats like there was sand in their mouths. It was just wrong. Onions-in-ice-cream wrong.

I could have been a rowboat cut loose from a dock, ropes dragging in the water as the current pulled me out to sea. Don't have the funeral? Don't finish the school year? Just disappear?

Rules. Can you just ignore them all? Apparently. When you get told you can't finish your English report. When it doesn't matter what your class rank is or where you might go to college. When all that matters is living through the day.

This was a nightmare—a nightmare, but so real. *Wake me up!*

"Dad?"

The grown-ups stopped talking. I didn't realize they'd been talking until they stopped.

"What is it, honey?"

"Can we go home now?" I talked just to him. One-on-one. I knew the others were there, but I was talking just to him. He'd listen to me.

He didn't answer me in that totally silent room.

"We can't go home?" I asked. "Just—just for tonight. Just—just for an hour. They won't know we went home. Not that fast. We can get Mom's knitting and her recipe books, at least. And some other things." What I wanted was her bathrobe. It smelled like her. I'd worn it before, so I knew. I wanted to put it on while it still smelled like her, and get that hug from those sleeves that had covered her arms.

Dad looked at the agents.

"Better not," said Mr. Oberman. "We'll pack everything and ship it to you."

No bathrobe, then.

No telephone calls, either, we were told. No e-mail. Nothing. We were advised not to be in touch with anybody that we ever knew. Not Aunt Peggy—well, Dad did call her from Ms. Harris's office, while Ms. Harris stood there and listened. While we waited for the marshals to be ready for us outside.

"I'm sorry, Peg," he kept saying. "I'm so sorry. . . . I don't know. I don't know. . . . So you'll handle the funeral? What? . . . Oh, just tell them the truth. Why not? We're hiding. Why lie about it? I'm sorry, but I don't know. I know we'll see you again. Sometime." He held the phone out to me.

"Aunt Peggy?"

"Oh, Liza!"

Then Dad took the phone back and finished saying good-bye to his only sister.

And she was the last person in our old life we would call. If we knew what was good for us.

Chapter 6

Dad gave Mr. Oberman all his IDs and his cell phone.

"We need your computer, too," said Ms. Harris. "You can't use this computer anymore."

Dad's eyes widened. "You want my *computer?*"

"I'm sorry. You could be found through it."

"But my research. I've got five years of research on there."

"We'll put it on a flash drive for you," said Ms. Harris. "We'll give you another laptop, and you should be good to go."

Dad just shook his head and handed the machine over to her, his lips grim. Ms. Harris took it and left the room. I didn't like his lips like that, so straight and thin. He looked at me, and the line went into a slight downturn on each side while he shook his head some more.

Mr. Oberman held his hand out again, this time to me. "I need your IDs too," he said. "Your cell phone."

"I don't have any IDs," I said, "and my cell phone's at home."

"Nothing's in your purse? Not even a school ID?"

"It's in another wallet," I said. "In my backpack."

"What about your learner's permit?"

"Same place."

"You don't have your *permit* with you?" Mr. Oberman didn't believe me. "What kid goes around without his permit?"

I opened my wallet and showed him the empty interior. No money or anything. "This kid," I said.

"Oh, Liza," said Dad. "Not even two dollars in there? What if you got into a jam somehow?"

I shrugged. "Anyway, I don't have my permit here."

"It doesn't matter," said Mr. Oberman. "We'll find it in your backpack along with your student ID and destroy it."

Good luck, I thought, because I knew where my permit really was. In my shoe. And I wasn't giving it up.

It was mine, with my name and my picture on it, taken right before Mom and I had gone out and bought a huge stuffed giraffe for her second-grade classroom. I was keeping it!

"Will I get another one?"

"Eventually."

Ms. Harris came back. "Ready?"

I looked around the room. "Ready for what?"

"The marshals are outside with the car."

"But what about our IDs?" asked Dad. "You took everything. We're nobody now."

We're nobody?

"One thing at a time," said Mr. Oberman. "You'll have new IDs soon."

"Come on." Ms. Harris gestured toward the door. "There's no time to lose."

Dad took my arm and squeezed it. "Let's go, Liza Jane."

We left the room with Mr. Oberman and Ms. Harris on either side of us, and took the elevator down. When we left the elevator, four other people, all tall, surrounded us.

"Dad!" I hung back. What was this? Who were these people?

"It's okay." Ms. Harris's hand was on my arm. Mr. Oberman had Dad's. Did they think we might fall? "These are our colleagues. We're walking you straight out to the car together."

Someone opened the doors to the outside, and we went out. Long quick strides, but not running. *Gogogogogo!* Straight to a car with tinted windows and an open rear door. *Gogogogogo!* The agents crowded around us as—first Dad, then me—we slunk inside.

Barely inside and *slam!* The door closed behind us.

Ms. Harris and Mr. Oberman and the other anonymous people watched us as the car started to move.

"Why?" I asked. "Why like that? Why so fast? No one knows we're here."

"We don't know that." A man with a thatch of white hair and blue eyes turned around from the front passenger side. "Chances are good someone from the Core is here somewhere." He held his hand over the seat. "Jeffrey Allen, U.S. Deputy Marshal. How are you?"

"I'll tell you tomorrow." Dad shook the marshal's hand, and I waved, not really sure I wanted to touch a hand that had something to do with making us disappear from our lives.

"Our wonderful driver," Mr. Allen went on, "is U.S. Deputy Marshal Beatrice Fox. We all call her Foxy."

Ms. Fox smiled at us in the rearview mirror, a row of even white teeth under brown lips. Brown lips that almost matched brown skin that almost matched brown hair.

"Try to relax," she said in what my dad would have called a contralto. Even her voice was brown. A rich, friendly brown, if that makes any sense. But so what? "Everything's under control," she said. Friendly brown—what was that? Today what did that mean when all the pieces of my life were coming apart? A random friendly voice was just another thing that didn't belong anywhere.

"Foxy," I said. "You want us to call you Foxy?"

"Please do."

"And I'm Jeff," said her colleague. "Nothing formal here."

I looked around as Foxy maneuvered us out of the space. Not many people even walking on the sidewalk. Just cars and buses shifting around us like water around uprooted trees as we angled more and more into the lane. One of these drivers was after us? Or was it a passenger on a bus?

The motorcyclist I'd seen from the window on the eighth

floor crossed the street toward us. He dodged through the traffic like he'd done it a million times, and the cars seemed to know their dance steps around him, too. The motorcyclist gave our car a long look as we slid past him, but there was nothing in that look that marked him as anybody I should worry about. He was just somebody trying to make it to the other side of the street. Trying to get to his motorcycle. No big deal. Except that he was there.

Did he have a gun in his pocket? Or was he merely a regular guy running errands and he just happened to be at that spot at that moment? Was it such a crime to take a long look at our car? But just in case, I memorized his features: curly black hair streaked with gray, thick black eyebrows, blue eyes, and freckled fair skin. A bar of music was tattooed above his right wrist.

How did I have time to take all that in? But time wasn't acting the way it always had.

Maybe it wasn't the motorcyclist who was after us. Maybe it was a sniper marking us from a window on the seventeenth floor across the street. Who knew? But . . . well . . . maybe it isn't so easy to stand in just any office window with a drawn gun. Wouldn't someone first say, *Who are you? Why are you here?* But what if—

My heart raced.

Stop it, Liza! You're making this all up. Stop!

"If someone was watching us as we came out," Dad asked, "how do you know no one's following us?"

"Somebody probably is," Foxy answered calmly, "and we're going to get rid of whoever that is."

"We're good at this," Jeff's voice assured us. "Have a little faith."

Dad and I looked at each other. Faith? When everything we'd ever taken for granted was gone? Faith? How do you have faith in the normal order of things when there is no longer any order to anything? Faith? What was that?

Then we started going in and out of some funny places. A school parking lot, a side street with a lot of vendors and pedestrian traffic and honking horns, then an intersection we sped through as a yellow light turned red. I looked back, and a tractor trailer blocked any other drivers from following us or even seeing where we went.

"That should do it," said Foxy, and shortly after that we were on a high-speed road. "We'll still pay attention, but I don't think anybody can have us pinpointed now."

"Where are we going?" asked Dad.

Oh, yeah. I hadn't even thought about where we were going, just where we were leaving. Just the getting out, getting out, getting out. Where to didn't seem to matter. But the car was pointed toward somewhere.

"Sea Isle City."

A place we'd been, at least, for day trips. And once when I was little, we'd spent a whole week there. I remembered saltwater taffy from that stay. Saltwater taffy and hot sand under my feet. And laughter.

No laughter now as light poles flashed by. All I could think was, *This isn't happening, this isn't happening.* Time passed, but I couldn't feel it, traveling in and out of trancelike states. *This isn't happening, this isn't happening.*

"U.S. Marshals?" asked Dad after a long silence. "They said you were marshals when we were getting ready to leave, but I didn't— I mean, I thought agents—marshals—it was the same. It's not, is it? You're not FBI agents."

"Nope," said Jeff. "We work for the U.S. Marshals Service. Marshals work with the FBI on these cases, though, protecting the bureau's witnesses. We're good at it, so we do it."

Dad was muttering. "The police, the FBI, the U.S. Marshals Service. What next?"

"I think that about covers it," said Foxy.

I felt Dad take a deep breath and let it out again, but he didn't say anything else.

"I guess we're doing what we need to do," I said to him, sort of to make him feel better, but it was Jeff who intercepted my comment and answered.

"Indeed you are."

We fell into another silence that felt like it would go on and on forever. Forever we'd be in the back of this car, forever we'd hear the hum of its engine, forever we'd speed through time and space, and there would be nooooo eeeeennnnd.

Stop.

A sign—PATHWAYS MOTEL—labeled the building next to us. We got out of the car.

"Shouldn't we run?" I saw nobody under that bright sunshine except a barefoot woman carrying a sleeping baby. Nobody else. Not where we were. And I just couldn't believe that woman was a threat to anybody. Deep breath in, deep breath out.

"We're okay now," said Foxy. "No need to run." She popped the trunk, and Jeff removed a laptop and my purse from it and handed them to us.

"A computer already?" asked Dad.

"The FBI can be fast," said Jeff. He took a flash drive out of his pocket and gave it to Dad. "Should be everything you need."

Then we were inside the motel, in a suite—number 101—with a view of the parking lot, a drippy sink in the bathroom, and just nothing friendly about it. Safe, though. That's what the marshals said. Safe.

"Want some water, Liza?" I looked, and Foxy held a glass out to me.

"Not thirsty." I didn't want anything. I just wanted to go home.

"Drink it anyway," she said. "You must be thirsty."

So I drank it, not caring if I did, staring, staring out that motel window at cars and weeds. Dad and the marshals talked. I didn't care. Whatever. If they weren't going to tell us how we could go home again, I didn't care what they said.

I stared down at the cars from the window. I could drive one of those cars. I could drive it right home. All I needed was for someone to say, *Want to borrow my car?* And I'd know what to do with it. Sure. I could drive. And someone would certainly ask that question. Right.

Foxy tapped me on the shoulder, and I turned around. "What?"

"Let's go," she said. "We'll take a look at the ocean and breathe the salt air."

Fine with me.

Fine.

Sort of fine.

Not fine.

No.

Leave Dad? I couldn't leave Dad.

"I get flashbacks," I explained. "I get flashbacks of when Mom died. If I'm with Dad, they stay away."

"Go ahead," said Dad. "You'll be all right."

"Can't you come too?"

"I want to see if everything's okay with this computer. I think I better speak now if there's a problem with it."

"But—"

"I'll be right here, and you can always come back if you're bothered. Go take a look at the water. Pick up some shells."

"All right." But I knew. I'd get as far the hall, and there Robert Bramwell would be. I'd get ten feet from the door, and I'd have to come back. So it didn't matter what I said.

I wasn't leaving.

Chapter 7

I was wrong.

Sure, Robert Bramwell was out there, hovering, hovering, but pushed away somehow. Stuck just out of sight. *Stay there*, I told him.

Foxy and I left the motel and took the sidewalk toward the center of town. "We'll find you a hat first," she said. "Get something to hide your hair before we hit the beach."

"I need to hide my hair?"

"Because it's that red color. It really makes you stand out."

"But there's no one here to care."

"It's best to be cautious."

And in a minute a shop with colorful T-shirts and bathing suits and pictures of sailing ships pulled Foxy inside. I followed.

"Oh, look!" Foxy held up a big straw hat with miniature

kites and streamers floating away from the brim. I didn't really want it, but she put it on my head, saying, "Come on. It will distract you."

How couldn't it? All those tiny orbits against my face—it took concentration just to walk with that going on around my eyes. Foxy bought one for each of us, and grinned up at me through the hanging mess of hers before we returned to the brightness of the sidewalk. *Clank, clink, tinkle, clank!* The decorations banged against my nose and cheeks. *Clank!*

This was so silly.

I held back a giggle. Or was it a sob?

"Lookin' good," Foxy said. "Can you stick the hair underneath a little more?"

Foxy said more, but I didn't catch what. Not with all those cars going by, people talking, the wind gusting, while I couldn't decide what pushed on my gut—a laugh or a cry. *Clank, clink, tinkle, clank!*

What happened to Mom hadn't really happened. We were away from it, and it was like a virus that would be cured before we got back. All offstage information I didn't need to know that would be taken care of, would cure itself, and then everything would be okay. *Just don't go back until it's done.*

I knew this wasn't true, but on Mars anything is true. Or everything. I wasn't sure which. But I knew I was on Mars, a place outside the bubble of earthlike truths.

Jabberjabberjabberjabber. Foxy went on and on. Something about my hair. I pushed it behind my ears and made a loose braid out of it. Stuck it under the back of my shirt. There. No more about the hair.

The wind whipped our hat decorations into noisy, colliding pinwheels. Foxy stilled some of her worst offenders with a hand and giggled. I didn't join her. No giggling allowed. "What's your favorite ice cream?" she asked me. Giggling could lead to sobs. Or vice versa. No sobs. No giggles.

"Oh." The wind tried to lift my hat away, but I clamped my hands around the cloth band. "Butter pecan. But you don't have to get me any."

I dropped my hands to my side. No more wind, and, after all, you can't keep your hands stuck to your head all the time.

The wind returned with a roar, and off went my hat. Foxy's giggles chased me as I took off after it. Each time I reached for it, the wind took it again, until it flattened three feet up from the pavement onto the wall of one of the shops. I grabbed the monstrosity away from the bricks, rolled my hair into a ball, and jammed the hat over it into what was now a tight fit. Victory! This hat wasn't going anywhere now!

I turned around and—Wham!—smacked right into something solid.

"Whoa!" A deep voice from the something solid. I grabbed him so he wouldn't fall, so I wouldn't fall. "Who-o-*oa*!"

I held him until he stopped reeling, I stopped reeling. A guy a little older than I was, but not as tall, and not as cute as Jellyfish. Cute, though. I let go. "Sorry. Sorry."

He stared at me, and I blushed. "It's okay," he said. He had a dimple on his left cheek that appeared and disappeared as he spoke. "It's okay." It turned out I hadn't quite let go, a fact I realized when he pulled my left hand off his arm. I blushed again. He smiled at me. "Nice hat," he commented, and then he disappeared around the corner. That half-sob, half-giggle pushed a little higher toward my throat.

No. No giggling. No giggling allowed.

Where was Foxy? She wasn't where I'd left her. I looked up and down the street.

Well, I was only two blocks from our motel. *See? There it is. The place with the white pillars.* I could go back there anytime I wanted. That's probably where she went. That was it. She'd lost sight of me while I chased my hat, and I'd find her at the motel, probably annoyed at me for disappearing. I could just go back. That would be the simplest thing. The best thing.

I didn't do that.

Who wanted to go there? Not me. The virus couldn't be cured if I went back.

Instead, even though I knew all my thoughts about the virus were nuts, I sat down on a nearby bench and waited—what for, I wasn't sure—watching the cars, watching the people, watching the flapping banners. I watched everything through the silliness of tiny orbits. Silly. Funny.

Nothing's funny! Don't laugh. Don't.

My shoulders shook, but I wasn't sure what from, tears or laughter. Where was Foxy? Shouldn't I be scared? Wasn't I scared?

A woman and her toddler crossed the street. Funny. A man going by whistled the *Star Wars* theme. Funny. A car made a U-turn. Funny.

I smiled, and then I was laughing silently.

Don't laugh.

Laughing out loud.

I should go back to the motel.

Laughing harder and harder.

No. Not going back. Never going back.

Better to laugh here on this bench than to go back where grim reality was as thick as pea soup and three times the earth's gravity. Better to be outside giggling like a maniac, as long as the guy in the U-turning car wasn't Gary Carmichael. Was he? I watched him. He was bald, but no. Probably not. Maybe not.

I couldn't see him, really, not well enough to tell. Well, of course it wasn't Gary Carmichael, anyway. Gary Carmichael wasn't real, so he *couldn't* be the guy doing the U-turn. He wasn't real. None of this was. I wasn't real, and neither was the laughter coming out of my mouth. Nobody could hear it because it wasn't real, but I could certainly feel the shake of my shoulders.

Someone sat next to me. The guy I'd almost knocked down. "You okay?"

Apparently you could hear my ha-ha's after all. I stopped it, swallowed it down to my gut. "Oh, sure," I said, and choked once. "Everything in my life is fine. Just fine. Peachy, peachy fine-line." Whatever that meant. I pushed down the next sob. I was real, after all. And this total stranger cared. *No giggling! Stop!*

"Liza?" Foxy stood before us with a cone in each hand.

"Boy," said the kid, "another one of those hats." He had a funny accent, and he talked more slowly than I was used to.

Foxy smiled. "Get one before they're gone."

"I'll do that," he said.

"Maxwell!" A man in a Cleveland Indians hat and a cigar between two fingers stood at the corner staring at us. "Come on!"

The boy rolled his eyes at me. "Maxwell," he muttered. He stood up and disappeared with the Indians fan.

Foxy sat down in his place. "Who was that?" she asked.

"Maxwell."

"Who?"

"I don't know. I almost knocked him down when I was chasing my hat. That's all I know about him. I think he thought I was homeless or something, the way I was sitting here laughing at nothing."

"I saw you laughing. Are you okay?"

"Where did you go?" I asked. "I didn't know where you were, and everything got feeling weird, so I kind of lost it."

"I was right over there." She indicated a walk-up counter about twenty feet away. "I called to you, and I thought you saw me."

"No."

"Don't worry. I won't lose sight of you, and I won't disappear. And chasing a hat halfway down a block doesn't constitute either one of us getting lost."

I sighed. "Okay."

"Here." Foxy handed me one of the cones. It was already starting to melt. "They didn't have butter pecan, so I got you butter brickle."

"Thanks." I took a lick. Such delicious coldness! When had I last eaten? I couldn't remember. Was it the toast with apricot preserves? Had I eaten that? I remembered spreading the preserves over the toast, but had I eaten it? I must have. Maybe. I took another lick. Was that today? "Very good," I added.

Foxy nodded at me. Then she cocked her head. "What beautiful eyebrows," she said. "I've never seen such a red. Almost black, but with that red shine."

"Yeah," I said. "I'm a conglomeration of weird genes."

"Oh, aren't we all?"

We finished our cones and just watched the traffic until Foxy's cell phone rang.

"Yes? Okay. On our way." She clicked the phone shut and looked at me. "Time to head back," she said.

We stood up. "We're going home?" I asked. "Back to Avon?"

"No. Something's up, and we have to get back to the motel. Come on. We better hurry."

"But we didn't see the ocean yet."

"Later for that."

Together we jogged up the sidewalk. The little mobiles smacked against my cheeks. *Clink, clank, clink!*

Why were we in a hurry? Why could we sit there on the bench like we had all the time in the world, and now be in a hurry?

What could have happened back at the motel? *Clink, clank!*

"Is something wrong?"

All Foxy did was shake her head, which did not give me a real good feeling.

"What is it?" I persisted. "Dad's okay, right?"

"Your dad's fine."

Then, what wasn't?

The sight of the motel's entrance brought me an edgy feeling, and the feeling increased, the closer we got to it. By the time we entered, my hands were shaking. Robert Bramwell's ghost aimed at me from just inside the lobby.

Bang!

Dad! I had to get to Dad!

Bang! Fall. *Bang!* Fall.

I sped up and turned a corner, colliding with the Indians hat man.

"Sorry," I said to him, but I didn't stop, just spun away, running harder and harder. By the time I could see the door to suite 101, I was in a full sprint. *Bang! Bang!*

"Hey! Wait!" Foxy was running behind me. I could hear her steps covering the carpeted floor, but I didn't wait. Wait? Are you kidding? *Bang!* I had to outrun that gun. *Bang!*

I made it to that door, and I knocked on it hard. "Dad! Dad!" *Knock, knock, knock, knock!* "Dad!"

Foxy came up beside me with the key card in her hand. "What's the matter?" The door opened right as she inserted the card into its slot.

There was Dad, and I put my arms right around him, my eyes squeezed tight.

I felt the outline of Robert Bramwell's ghost come apart and evaporate. When I opened my eyes, he was gone. I pushed away from Dad and looked around to see, to make sure. Just gone.

"Okay?" Dad asked. He took off my silly hat and my released hair fell all over my face and shoulders. "I like your hat." He put it on himself.

He looked so ridiculous, I couldn't help but grin at him. "It is kind of fun, isn't it?"

"What happened?" Foxy's eyes were wide, and her hat clanked between her hands.

"Was there a problem?" Jeff appeared on the edge of the action. I guessed he'd been there all along, but I hadn't seen him. I hadn't been looking for him either. Just Dad. And Dad was okay.

"I was having a flashback," I explained. "I'm all right now." I let out a good breath. "Now I'm okay."

We entered the suite, and I sat down on the sofa, still breathing hard. Okay? I didn't feel so okay. Dad took the spot beside me and clasped my hand. He was still wearing the silly hat, but I could see the hat was beside the point now. I didn't think he even remembered he was wearing it.

"Is something the matter?" I asked him. Because Dad never just sat down beside me and held my hand. I took the hat off his head and tossed it onto the coffee table. *Clank, clink!* It hit a glass ashtray. "Why'd we have to get back here so fast?"

Dad half-shrugged. "I'm sorry," he said, "but Gary Carmichael's in Sea Isle City."

There was a pause. A huge pause. One you could drive a truck through, a tractor trailer through, a 747, or a moon. The whole universe.

Gary Carmichael in Sea Isle City? Same as we were? Same as we were, maybe buying ice cream or taking a walk along the water? In a motel, maybe? In this motel? I could have run into *him* instead of the Cleveland Indians guy. How come I didn't? Or would I the next time I left the suite?

What kind of stuff was this? Weren't the marshals supposed to be making us safe?

"But," I said, putting my finger on the flaw, as though that mattered, "if he was spotted, why wasn't he arrested? And how do you know, anyway?"

"He's slippery," said Jeff. "That's all I can tell you. He got away. Gary Carmichael is someone who always knows how to get away."

"He must know Dad and I are here," I said. "How can he know that?"

Jeff shook his head. "That, I can't say. But here's the deal. We have to leave Sea Isle City, and we have to leave now."

Chapter 8

"Not from Philadelphia," Foxy said before we left the motel. "Too obvious to fly from there." She handed me a rich lady's turban. Silky white with sequins, her quick purchase while Jeff'd made some phone calls. "Wear this."

"You're kidding."

"You need to hide your hair. And the hat won't work for the plane."

So I put it on. If that wasn't ridiculous. Me in a turban? *That* didn't make me stand out?

"Keep it on until you get there," she said. "Then you might want to dye your hair another color."

Dye my hair? I wasn't dyeing anything! But I didn't say so.

"Just for the flight," said Jeff, "your names are Lydia and Horace Williams. Can you remember that? Horace and Lydia."

Dad and I repeated our new names. I was a Lydia?

"We'll have temporary cards for you for the airport." Jeff looked at Foxy.

She nodded. "Mamie will be at departures with them when we get there," she said. "All in place."

"Those temporary IDs won't mean anything once we're in the air," said Dad. "We'll be nobodies for sure."

"Not to us," said Foxy. "We know who you are."

"And you will get different IDs once you land," Jeff said.

"You and Foxy aren't coming with us?" asked Dad.

"I am," said Foxy. "I'll hand you over to the marshal on the other end, and then I'll say good-bye."

We left the motel and went to Newark Liberty International Airport. All the way in New Jersey.

"Good luck to you," said Jeff when we got out of the car at departures. He handed me an iPod. "You'll want this for the flight."

"You're giving me an iPod? I can't take that."

"It's all right," he said. "My brother gave me this one when he upgraded, but I like my other one better." He pressed it on me. "Take it. He's got a lot of good music on it."

"But—"

"Think of it as a loan," he said. "When you come back to the area, you can return it to me."

So I took it, and Foxy was right there, returning from somewhere I hadn't even noticed her going. "Okay, everybody?" She handed Dad and me our new cards. According to mine I was a licensed driver from Arizona. Same picture as on my learner's permit, but the hair was black. "Mamie was right on time."

We said good-bye to Jeff and moved on through security. No problems at all, even if I was black-haired Lydia Williams from Arizona. I sure didn't look like a Lydia, black-haired or otherwise. But maybe Lydias wore rich-lady turbans.

We got through security and immediately boarded a plane. How safe was that, even with Foxy in the aisle seat next to Dad? No place to go unless we jumped out, which was what I wanted to do. Jump out and fall into Neverland, where life was all cream puffs.

But one of Jeff's calls had been to make sure we were in the back of the plane, so we were probably as safe as anyone could make us. Plus I was way against the window, me and my turban. No one was going to see me, but if they did, they'd laugh. They might not pick up on the red hair, but they'd laugh. Oh, well. Go ahead and laugh.

And where were we going? I hadn't thought of that until we were actually at the airport. Somebody must have said it or asked it or something, but it hadn't registered until we were practically on the plane. Until then it was all about leaving, and the destination didn't matter. What difference could the destination make?

Wichita.

Wichita?

Wichita, yes, as in *Kansas*.

Kansas!

Not a real place. Imaginary. Like Siberia and New Zealand and the north pole. All places on the map that weren't real. Places people said were real, even lied about and said they'd been to and all that, but they weren't real. I mean, have you ever known anyone from *Kansas*?

The flight felt real enough with the safety talk, and the seat belt pulled across my lap, and the small snatches of conversation overheard against the engines' hum. The takeoff and the being in the air felt real enough, but where were we going? *Wichita?* Right. Sure. Uh-huh.

Up in the air, up in the air, up in the air. How could anybody tell we were even moving? Just white, white, white out there. Maybe all we were doing was hovering over Newark, and after the clouds wore away, we'd float down again. Uh-huh.

Landing in Wichita made about as much sense to me as landing on an island of raisins in a giant bowl of Cream of Wheat.

I turned away at some point from the mashed-potato clouds. "I'm in la-la land," I told Dad.

He nodded and rolled his eyes. "Who isn't?"

Foxy turned and smiled at me. "Hang in there," she said.

She went back to watching the aisle, Dad went back to his magazine, and I turned on the iPod, trying not to think. *Music, music, music.* I upped the sound and sank into it over my head.

It was a long time before we landed in Wichita, time interspersed with real things like flight attendants offering us snacks, the stopover in Chicago, and sometimes just having to think about Mom and our exile from Pennsylvania, whether I wanted to or not. Tears would take over once in a while, and I just didn't know what to do about that except *music, music, music.* That was where I went.

During the stopover I walked into a pillar—*Bonk!*—because I was listening too hard to the iPod.

Foxy came running, and Dad grabbed me as I reeled. "Are you all right?"

"Oh, I'm fine." I put the iPod away, but I sure felt stupid and embarrassed. Who walks into pillars?

"Don't worry about it," said Dad. "Once I stepped off a dock because I was reading."

"Really?"

"No. But I could."

"Oh, Dad."

Our flight was called soon after that, and up in the air we were again. I did a whole bunch of puzzles in a book we'd bought in O'Hare, while I listened to Jeff's brother's music again. It didn't make me believe in Wichita or Kansas, but it helped me not think.

Finally we landed in Wichita. I put the iPod away so I wouldn't walk into any more pillars, and the three of us got off the plane behind a bunch of other people who didn't look like they expected Wichita to be a raisin island in a bowl of Cream of Wheat or anything except the usual city kinds of things. And they were right. It was real, just like all those liars had said. Real.

We walked into a waiting area.

"Ms. Fox?"

A man in a gray suit stood nearby. He held out a badge. "Walter Swensen, U.S. Marshals Service."

Foxy showed her badge to him. "Good to meet you," she said. He took from her a bag of items she'd purchased for us during our stopover in Chicago. Pajamas, combs, toothpaste, and toothbrushes. That kind of thing.

Then she shook Dad's hand and gave me a quick hug.

"Good luck," she said, and headed for her return flight.

I watched her receding back. Brown hair, brown skin, brown lips, brown voice. I'd liked her. I probably would never see her again.

"Okay." Mr. Swensen's voice brought me back to where I stood. "Harvey and Linda Weston, welcome to Wichita."

I looked at Dad. "What?"

"That must be who we are now," said Dad. "Good to meet you," Dad said to the marshal. The two men shook hands.

Linda. I was now Linda. No more Lydia, no more Liza. I was Linda. No, I wasn't! No matter what anybody said!

After a short conversation we followed Mr. Swensen to the outside darkness.

"Ten o'clock at night," commented Dad.

"A long day," I answered.

Mr. Swensen took us through hot, windy air to a red Subaru with Kansas plates. All the cars around it also had Kansas plates. Not a single one from Pennsylvania, which was what I wanted to see. Just one.

Dad took the seat next to the marshal, and I sat in the back, where I could keep my eye on Dad. It wasn't like he was going anywhere, but I needed to see him. Just keep making sure he was there.

"So," Dad asked, "what's next?"

Mr. Swensen pulled the car out of its space. "What's next," he said, "is a trip to the hotel." He maneuvered through the lot to the exit and onto the road.

I looked out the window while Mr. Swensen and Dad made small talk. "How was the trip?" "Fine." "Any problems?" "None at all." I concentrated on the road, trying not to listen.

One thing I noticed on the drive to the hotel. Everywhere you looked, the land was flat. How could everything be so flat? Somehow I was keyed to brace against the next hill, the next curve, the next something, and there just wasn't one. It didn't seem right to never feel even a slight rise in the road. With each non-curve and non-hill, I felt the suspense grow. I needed *one*, anyway. *One!*

Another driver cut suddenly in front of us.

Hooonk! Swe-e-erve! We half-circled the other car. *There* was a curve I could lean into! Stupid driver, but I was glad. For a second.

"Sorry." Mr. Swensen glanced in the rearview mirror at me. "You okay?"

Hooooonk!

I looked backward. Another car was swerving around the lane changer, who'd stopped. Just stopped. What the heck? Why would you just stop on the highway? The second car kept on honking—*What's he doing? What's he doing?*—then swerved in front of *us* before—I held my breath—almost clipping our left fender.

Mr. Swensen slammed on the brakes. "Jerk!" he shouted. The other driver veered away to an exit ramp. "Jerk. *Jerk!*"

"You've got bad drivers here, too, have you?" asked Dad.

"Nobody has a monopoly on them." Mr. Swensen's voice was still tense.

Dad looked back at me. "Everything all right?" he asked.

"I feel a little scared, that's all."

"Perfectly normal," said Mr. Swensen.

But it didn't feel normal to me. I mean—the second driver—he was just a bad driver, right? And he was gone, right? What was there to be afraid of? But he had almost clipped us. Had it been on purpose? Was he from the Core?

We kept on, and nothing else happened before we got to the hotel. Just an ordinary piece of driving, nobody doing anything odd or threatening. That second driver. He was just a bad driver. Had to be.

Mr. Swensen stopped the Subaru in a parking lot. BLUE MOON HOTEL glowed the blue script letters on the side of the building.

"Well, here we are," said Mr. Swensen, and he opened his door.

I stepped out of the car. The sun was down, but the air felt stiflingly hot, even worse than at the airport. No wind to make it better here.

"How do you breathe this?" I asked.

Mr. Swensen grinned at me. "You got us during a heat wave," he said. "It'll ease up." He led us into the cooled hotel. "Ahh. Much nicer." Dad and I followed him down a hallway before he opened a door and ushered us into a suite. "Welcome to your new digs."

Mm. Two bedrooms, a living room, and a bathroom. Not fancy, not home, and not even a kitchen. At least it didn't look out onto a parking lot like the place in Sea Isle City had, but I still didn't like it. Sea Isle City. From there I could have at least driven home in a couple of hours. Or maybe one of my friends could have just *happened* to turn up. But Wichita? Forget it.

"I hate this place," I said.

"It's just temporary, Linda," Mr. Swensen said to me. Linda. Linda Weston. *Pleased ta meecha.*

"The place is all right, I guess," I said. Linda said. Me said. "I just wish I could go home."

Mr. Swensen talked to us for a few more minutes. We were now from Beverly, a small town in Burlington County, New Jersey, that was right on the Delaware.

"You went to Palmyra High School," he told me, "because Beverly's school goes only to eighth grade. When we get your school transcripts sent, they will say Palmyra."

"Why'd we move?" asked Dad.

"You can come up with that," said Mr. Swenson.

"Because Mom died," I said, "and home was too sad a place to stay."

Dad looked at me. "That's pretty much the truth."

"Then it's a story that should be pretty easy to remember," said Mr. Swensen. And then he gave Dad a cell phone.

"I'm speed dial one," he said.

"Thanks," said Dad. "You're not staying here?"

Mr. Swensen shook his head. "You should be okay as long as you keep a low profile. But definitely call me the instant you have a concern."

"I thought we'd have round-the-clock protection."

"You would if we thought you were in a high-threat situation, but no one knows you're here. And I'm only as far away as your phone." Then he handed Dad a wad of cash.

"Whoa!" Dad thumbed through it. "This should take care of a few breakfasts."

"That's until we have your stipend set up," said Mr. Swensen. "You'll get a bank card for that in a few days." He held out some keys. "They're for a gray Caravan. It'll be in the parking lot in the morning, in the last space before the exit. It'll be yours. And your car registration and IDs and bank cards for access to the money from your previous accounts will all be in there. New names, new numbers. If there's anything missing, it's just because it can take some time."

"Hm," said Dad. "A gray Caravan. And to think that this morning—was that only this m—" He stopped and bit his lip. "Thanks. We're glad to have wheels."

At least it wouldn't be that red Subaru that had brought us here. Not after that skirmish on the road. If that crazy driver who did that was from the Core, maybe he'd look for us in that red Subaru, which was a good reason not to have Mr. Swensen hanging around with it. Of course, maybe that crazy driver was just a crazy driver and we'd never see him again. But how could you know?

"So now we have a van," Dad said. "I've never owned one of those."

"What about the Buick and the Honda? When do we get them?" I liked driving Mom's Honda. Small and easy to maneuver. And it had that red rose pin she'd fastened to one of the sun visors. A present from one of her second graders.

"We're done with the Honda and the Buick," said Dad.

"What?"

"They're traceable to you," said Mr. Swensen.

"We can't have them anymore? What's going to happen to them?"

"We're selling them. Same as your house."

"*What?* You're selling our *house?*"

"It's all right, Liza." Dad glanced at Mr. Swensen. "Linda, I mean. It's the deal. I should have told you already."

"But our house, Dad."

"I know. I don't like it either."

Man! I stood there shaking my head. Man! Did we have to lose everything? *Man!*

"I'll let you know when they need you in Pennsylvania," Mr. Swensen was continuing. "I'll take care of the arrangements when you have to fly back."

Susan Shaw

"When will that be?" I asked. The house, the cars, what else? Our hands? Our noses? Our front teeth? I took off the turban and shook out my hair. With everything else feeling more and more restricted, it felt good at least to free my hair.

He shrugged. "They haven't caught the guy yet, right? It could be a while." He looked at me, considering.

"What?"

"Did anybody tell you to dye your hair?"

I touched it. "Foxy—Ms. Fox suggested it. I don't want to."

"Do it. Keeping it red makes it easier to identify you. And that is an unusual shade of red, so you'll really stand out with it if you leave it alone."

"But you said nobody knows we're here," said Dad. "That's why you're not giving us round-the-clock protection. So what difference can it make what color her hair is?"

"It's still best to play it safe," Mr. Swensen said. "You don't need to actually draw attention to yourself."

I brought my hand down slowly. "But—my mother's hair's the same color. *Was* the same color." It would be wrong, taking that color away. My hair—her hair.

Mr. Swensen nodded curtly, and I didn't like him. "Take my advice. Dye it."

Then he left, and Dad and I were on our own.

"I'm not dyeing my hair, Dad," I told him. "I can't. It's the only way I take after Mom."

"Your call," he said. "We'll buy you a big hat for the time being. You can hide your hair in that. Or that turban."

The turban! Like I was going to wear that again. I squinted at him.

He answered the squint. "Better than being killed."

"I'm never dyeing my hair," I said, "and those guys aren't looking for me, anyway. The Core! Right. Why would they care about me? It was all a mistake. They're certainly not going to come all the way out here to find me, when it was just a mistake."

"I'm too tired to argue," said Dad, "and right now, red, yellow, purple, I don't care what color your hair is as long as you're breathing under it. Shave it, for all I care." His voice rose as he went on. "Cover it with chocolate mousse. Curl it with ice cubes. Fly it to Peru."

"Dad, I'm sorry."

He closed his eyes for a second and shook his head. Then he put his arm around me. "It's okay," he said, although his voice was still a little high. "Right this minute you can't dye your hair anyway, and I really don't care. The turban or a hat will be good enough. Now I want to crash. How about you?"

"Sounds like a plan."

He took one bedroom and I took the other, and that was it for the night.

Chapter 9

When I emerged at first light, Dad was staring out the window.

"Morning, Dad."

He turned. "Hey, Liza Jane. Hungry?"

"Starved."

"Then grab your gear."

"What gear?" I held up my bag from the coffee table. "You mean this? All that's in here is an empty wallet." I didn't mention the learner's permit I'd put back before going to bed.

He held out a twenty. "For that random ice cream cone," he said. "No one should ever have an empty wallet."

"I see the price for ice cream has gone up."

"Maybe Wichita has the best ice cream in the world, and people pay that much for it. You never know."

I grinned, but I took the twenty and stuck it into my wallet.

Dad picked up the turban I'd dropped on the coffee table the night before and handed it to me. "Ready, little one? Let's eat."

I put the wallet into my jeans pocket and shoved my hair into the turban, and we left the suite. Before going out to the van, though, Dad and I took a tour of the hotel, stopping at one point to look at the pool. Well, at least the hotel had one. Not that I had a bathing suit with me so I could use it. Neither of us had one. All we had were the few items Foxy had purchased for us to get through the night. Plus the teddy bear and the iPod and Dad's computer.

Dad and I stared at the pool. A lone paper cup floated in it, and no one was around except us.

"Nothing like a swim on a hot day," Dad said. "We'll buy some suits." He glanced at me. "Maybe a bathing cap for you."

"A bathing cap." I'd never worn one of those—I turned away from the water—and I didn't want to start. "What I could use is a clean outfit," I said, "but maybe a bathing suit wouldn't be a bad idea."

"Agreed," said Dad. "Let's go eat and then get some things. Then maybe we can relax around the pool."

So we went out to the van, which was right where Mr. Swensen had said it would be. It had a few dings on its bumper.

"Not a new car," said Dad, "but if it runs, I'm not going to argue."

I climbed in and, not liking my wallet between my hip and my seat belt, pushed my wallet under the seat. Who needed it anyway? I tilted the seat and leaned back, staring at the ceiling.

"All set."

"Hold on." Dad was beside me, looking through the IDs left in the glove compartment. "A driver's license for me is here, at least. You have a school ID from Palmyra High School."

I sat up. "What about my learner's permit?"

"No. We'll have to ask about that. And some of my bank cards would be handy to have."

"Mr. Swensen said it might take a little time." I dropped back again. "And I guess I could just get another learner's permit here myself. Why not?"

"That's the spirit." He started the van.

I didn't care. I had the Pennsylvania one, and for now that was the only one that mattered to me.

Dad steered us out of the parking lot and onto the streets of Wichita. Wichita! I blinked at the place. How could we be here when two days ago—

We found a place to eat and then bought some clothes—a pair of sandals for each of us, bathing suits, bathing cap for me (ugh!), and even a hat for each of us with the Phillies red *P* bright against the navy blue fabric.

"So we aren't so homesick," said Dad.

Mine was an oversize bucket hat that covered all of my hair except for what hung down below collar level. I rolled my hair into a bun, so even that much was undetectable.

"See?" I said to Dad. "Easy." I dropped the turban into one of the shopping bags. The end of that!

"As long as you like wearing hats," was his answer.

Then we just drove around, looking at the town.

"Wichita's not so bad," said Dad.

"It's okay." Maybe it would feel like home someday, although, right then, that did not seem possible.

The people on the sidewalks—none of them were like my friends or anyone I knew at all, no matter how hard I looked.

How was this place going to feel like home if nobody looked right? What I would have given just to see even Mr. Sprenkle, my old history teacher, whom I didn't even like and who made history sound as exciting as wet sand.

Eyebrows and chins and noses—they were all in the wrong places in the wrong shapes on the wrong faces.

"How can there be so many faces?" I asked Dad. "How come there aren't ever any duplicates? Not counting twins, I mean. How come we don't see repeats? Everybody's got two eyes and a nose and a mouth. There can't be that much variation. Those features have all got to be in sort of the same place."

And why can't somebody here look like Jackie or Mrs. Pomeroy or Jellyfish? I didn't have to see Mr. Sprenkle. Why was I looking for him?

"I guess you're right," said Dad. "You never see a pair of eyes under a nose. Good thing. Think how awful that would be if your nose was runny."

I giggled. "Sorry," I said, but I giggled again. I couldn't hold it down.

"It's all right." Dad smiled at me, and I felt better. "Mom

would want us to laugh. You know what she used to say? Not that we're doing it. She'd say for her funeral, hire a clown. Put up a piñata and have a party. Don't be sad."

"Maybe," I said, "if she'd lived to be old, really old, that's what we'd have done. Instead of this way, when we can't even go to the funeral, let alone hire a clown."

"Well, I guess we could still hire a clown," said Dad. "Seems kind of pointless, though, doesn't it?"

We drove back to the hotel and spent the rest of the day not doing much—sleeping, looking at television, reading the paper. Who had energy for anything? We didn't even bother with the pool.

In the evening Dad found a baseball game on television that wasn't the Phillies. We were so tired that just spacing out in front of that seemed like work.

"How do people do this?" I asked sometime during the game. We hadn't been talking, just letting the voices of the sports announcers wash over us. It didn't matter. Dad knew what I meant.

He put the TV on mute, and we talked while teams in whites and blues continued to soundlessly play.

"I don't know," he answered, "but they do it all the time. Most people don't have to leave their homes, friends, and jobs, though, when they lose loved ones. That makes it harder, but you and I, we'll figure it out."

"You haven't really lost your job at Temple, have you?"

"The university'll put me on leave, but I can't take another job like it before all this is settled. Too many people know me in the music world, and our cover would get blown, even if I used another name."

"So what are you going to do?"

"I'm going to finish that Stravinsky book. I never get enough time. Now I have time."

"But what about money?"

"Don't forget the Broadway show." He grinned at me. "There's always a chance it'll make us rich."

"I'd like to see it sometime."

"By hook or by crook," said Dad. "We'll sneak in. We'll wear Groucho Marx glasses and sneak in. Or you can be the front half of a horse, and I'll be the back half."

"Sure," I said. "That won't call any attention to us at all." I smiled at him because he wanted me to. "But just suppose your musical isn't a hit—"

"You don't like my three-flop track record?" he interrupted.

"They were funny shows," I said. "But, Dad—"

"We'll make it," he said. "The FBI will help us out. Remember Mr. Swensen talked about a stipend? That's what that means. It won't be a lot, but it will be something. And we have savings. Ever since I got laid off all those years ago, your mom and I saved for another emergency. Plus we have the royalties on the Bach book. Good thing so many colleges use it in the classroom. We'll get by."

"You make it sound like everything's all okay."

He shrugged again. "I wouldn't say it's all okay, but it's okay enough. We won't have to live under a bridge, and we won't go hungry. We can deal."

That was good, but Mom! We didn't have Mom! Being without her and starting completely over in an alien territory without Jackie, Jellyfish, my other friends, Aunt Peggy—it felt cold and moon-size. *Come on!* It wasn't fair!

"So, it's not fair," answered Dad when I said so. "Who are you gonna write a letter to?"

Write a letter. That's what he and Mom always said when I complained that something wasn't fair—a rainy day or a scraped knee or a boring teacher like Mr. Sprenkle. Write a letter. Go ahead. See what it gets you. And to whom? That was always the kicker. Who do you complain to about a skinned knee? Just clean up the blood and get over it. So it feels sore for a while. That's what happens when you skin your knee.

I made a face at Dad, but there wasn't much I could say.

He un-muted the TV. "Oh, a pitching change," he said, and flipped through the channels. *NCIS*, the Weather Channel, FOX News—

"Hey!" We said it together. A picture of Mom froze on the screen.

"—the murder of a forty-year-old second-grade teacher in Pennsylvania." *Mom!* Then it was her with her class, and then a picture of me on the basketball court. "No one knows what—"

Dad pushed mute again, then just actually turned the whole set off before throwing the remote across the room so it bounced against the wall. *Thunk!*

I stared at him. "But that was us."

"I'm not looking at it. I'm not looking at anything like that. It's bad enough we have to live through all this."

"But that was national news," I said. "Why are we on television? Why are they talking about Mom like she was famous?"

His head was in his hands. "A human interest story. Of all stories, they had to pick this one to make the public go 'Awwww.'" He looked up. "Can we have a deal? For right now?"

"Sure. What?"

"We don't look at any news, listen to any news, look at any newspapers. Not for a while."

"Dad? Are you all right?"

"No. I'm not all right. That's my wife they're selling cars with. My *wife*! I'm not going to make it if I have to look at stuff like that."

I put my hand on his shoulder. "It's a deal, Dad. It's a deal."

The next day was the funeral. At least we thought so. We went out to dinner that night and ordered Mom's favorite meal. Salmon and rice with a tomato salad.

Chapter 10

We stayed at the Blue Moon for a few weeks. It was near a lot of stuff, so we could walk to most things. We did a lot of that. Walking. We walked around the streets, read in the library. Went to the movies. Took the van to explore a wider area, but outside of Wichita, there wasn't much to look at besides farms. It didn't matter where we went. We always wore our hats.

On one of those trips we stopped someplace just to get out of the van. Cows and corn and a steady strong breeze. Hot. That was one thing I didn't like—how ovenlike the air was. How could people stand it all the time? Mr. Swensen had called it a heat wave, so maybe the air would cool down eventually. I turned my face into the breeze, let it pull the hair away from my face. It didn't feel like the breezes at the Jersey shore. So hot.

"Not bad," said Dad. "Not bad at all."

"It's hot," I said to him, "and flat. How do you get used to it?"

"People from Kansas probably go to Pennsylvania and say 'Look at all the hills.' They probably wonder how we can stand living with all of them. And so many trees."

"Yeah. They probably like having it so clear and flat. No secrets in Kansas. And think how they must save on ovens."

"Except for the oven part," said Dad, "I'm glad. It makes it harder for people to sneak up on us with everything out in the open."

Gary Carmichael had sneaked up on me in Avon, all right, and there hadn't been any big hills on our street to hide him. I just hadn't seen him. And he'd been sneaking up on us in Sea Isle City. How had he even known we were there? Did he know we were in Kansas? If he'd known we were at the shore, I asked Dad, wouldn't it make sense that he'd know we were now in Kansas? Not that I believed he was really looking for us. He was on vacation in the Bahamas and not thinking about us. He hadn't been in Sea Isle City at all, probably. It was all a mistake.

"No," said Dad. "He doesn't know we're here."

"How do you know?"

"We're still alive. If Carmichael knew where we were, we probably wouldn't be."

"But—"

"And if he was going to know, he would have known right away—maybe by following us to the airport somehow, seeing us get on the plane. But Jeff and Foxy were good. They protected us, and we got out of Sea Isle City without the Core finding out. Now, as far as the Core is concerned, we could be anywhere. Out of all the world, why look here?"

But what if something went wrong? What if somebody in the FBI told Carmichael where we'd gone? What if he just hadn't been able to take a flight to Wichita yet? What if later he could?

Would flat, treeless, duneless Kansas make it harder for him to track us down? The cornfield in front of us could hide him. Could he be in it? But even Gary Carmichael couldn't have known we'd be here, here in this exact spot at this exact moment. He couldn't be waiting for us right here right now. That was something.

I watched the cornstalks sway in the wind. So much corn . . .

But he wasn't looking for us. It was all a mistake. Nobody'd ever wanted to bother *us*!

"Okay, Liza," said Dad, and I didn't correct him. I was Liza no matter what anybody said. "Let's go."

"Can't take the heat, huh?"

"And I'm getting out of the kitchen." He opened my door, and I felt the leftover air-conditioning as I bent into my seat.

"Ahh, that's better."

We traveled a little more before coming upon a sign: COS- MOSPHERE: KANSAS COSMOSPHERE AND SPACE CENTER.

"What's this doing out here?" I asked.

"Well, why not? You don't have to be an Easterner to care about space travel."

He steered into the museum's driveway, and we parked.

"But who comes here? Cows?"

He gestured to the other cars in the parking lot. "I don't think they're driven by cows. I could be wrong about that. It's only my opinion. Maybe in the Midwest cows drive."

"Dad!"

So we went inside for a tour of the Cosmosphere. We took our time. There was no place we needed to be, so we figured we might as well learn all there was to learn about the lunar landing, look at the rocket ship the museum people had somehow managed to get there from wherever the astronauts had splashed down, and imagine what it might be like to shoot up into space in one.

"Not me," said Dad. "I like my feet on the ground."

"No tree climbing for you?" I asked.

I turned my head to see what was farther down the exhibit. A man and woman, a little girl, maybe four years old, her hand held by her father. Her father—

Gary Carmichael!

How could he just be standing there like a regular person, holding his daughter's hand while they studied the spaceship? How could he do that? I kept looking at him. Gary Carmichael. No doubt about it. Six feet tall, mostly bald with a blond fringe. And here?

"Not with this shoulder," Dad was answering.

I gripped Dad's arm and pulled. "Come on." I whispered, but my words weren't very audible, and they were mostly covered up by his.

"What? What's wrong?"

I pointed. "Gary Carmichael," I mouthed.

Dad's skin whitened around his lips. "Quietly, quietly," he whispered.

He pulled me toward him, and we slowly retreated.

I checked to make sure my hair was all inside my hat. Would it matter? If Gary Carmichael was here, then he knew I was too. How much would it matter if he saw my hair? But there was the doorway, and he hadn't turned around yet. We had to get only as far as the doorway, and— Why hadn't he turned? Was someone else waiting to grab us when we ran, as we surely would once we got out?

Or was Gary Carmichael waiting for just the right moment to pull out his gun—maybe when we reached the doorway— and then *bang!* No more questions.

Then Gary Carmichael did turn around and—*Oh, no! Oh, no!*—give us a look with somebody else's face of complete and total disinterest. He bent over the little girl to listen to her say something. Not Gary Carmichael. Not Gary Carmichael at all. He didn't even look like him, not with those eyebrows and their elfin slant.

"No," I said to Dad, and I rolled my eyes. "It's somebody else." I let out a deep breath. So did Dad. "I feel really stupid. Sorry."

The sort-of Gary Carmichael was fatter, too. How had I missed that? And would he really have brought his little girl along if he'd been getting ready to murder us? Right.

"It's okay," Dad said. "Understandable." He let out another deep breath. The skin around his lips returned almost to their usual color. And I let out another deep breath.

"Going to make it?" asked Dad.

"Oh, sure." I rolled my eyes again. "Are you?"

"Right there with you, little one." He led me back to where we'd been, and we studied the exhibit.

"Does your shoulder hurt today?" I wanted to take us back to where we had been. "That old car accident just doesn't go away, does it?"

I knew we both kept thinking it had been a close call. It hadn't been. This man wasn't Gary Carmichael, period, and he never had been. Not a close call. This man wasn't dangerous. Not even a little bit.

Gary Carmichael. Right. Uh-huh. I was just too ready to see him everywhere.

"It doesn't hurt," said Dad, climbing back in time with me, "but it might if I tried shimmying up a tree. So I'm not doing that. I probably couldn't anyway, even if I tried."

"Not many trees to shimmy in Kansas."

"Then Kansas is working out just fine."

I didn't know about Dad, but I personally didn't take in much at the museum after that almost-encounter. The sort-of Gary Carmichael made me nervous. Every time he turned his back, I believed he was the real thing, and my heart raced.

He could be Gary Carmichael. He might not still be the man with the funny eyebrows. They could have traded places when you weren't looking. It's possible. They could be brothers, and Gary Car—

Stop it!

The noise inside my head would end for a few minutes. Then up it would start again, and I practically had to pinch myself to keep reality real.

This man was *not* Gary Carmichael!

Not!

Dad and I finished the tour. There was no reason to hurry except for the *Go! Go! Go!* message my heart kept beating. But where would have been better? The hotel? I could invent Gary Carmichael there, too.

Calm down, calm down, I told myself. *Calm down.*

No one named Gary Carmichael was here. Nobody was here who'd even heard of Gary Carmichael, except Dad and me, and probably we were wrong. He didn't exist and was all made up out of papier-mâché.

The whole thing was made up, not just him.

Life still felt so unreal. Mom was dead, someone had attacked me with a knife, and now we were living in Kansas. How believable was any of that? I was going to come out at the end of some tunnel, I had to, and find I'd been walking through a giant bubble in an amusement park. A giant plastic bubble made up of all the worst nightmares with all the scariest colors. But it wouldn't be real.

Well, yeah.

At the exit, when we finally got to it, we hit the outside

air, and I sprinted for the van, steaming temperatures or not. I didn't care. I just wanted out of there.

"You in a race?" asked Dad when he caught up with me. "It's kind of toasty out here for the Penn Relays."

"I just didn't like being in there with that man."

"You could have said so."

I shrugged. "It was silly."

"It was not silly. Next time say it, and we'll turn on a dime. I didn't like him either."

We entered the Caravan, and Dad steered us out of the parking lot. I took off my hat. Too hot, and nobody was around.

"Where to?" I asked, but Dad was singing. He was singing, so I guessed everything was okay after the non-Carmichael scare. Why had we been scared? Gary Carmichael was never going to look for us. He was under a beach umbrella somewhere not caring about us at all. Dad was singing. That was what mattered.

"On the way to Cape Maaaay."

"Bum-bum-ba-bum." I provided the bass.

"La, la, la, la, with yooou."

"Can't remember the words?"

He grinned. "Words escape me, but I do know the tune."

"I wish we *were* on the way to Cape May. Not Sea Isle City. Not now. But Cape May's good. Nobody's looking for us there and probably never has been. And I wouldn't mind seeing the ocean, maybe getting some saltwater taffy, lying on the beach and eating it. Then going home when it was all gone. Wouldn't that be great?"

"Good thing I'm your father," said Dad.

"Why? Not that I dispute your statement."

"Because you need somebody to say no, you can't eat all that saltwater taffy at once. You'll get a stomachache."

"Dad!"

"We'll go there again," he said.

"Where? Home or Cape May?"

"Both. You'll see. We're just going through a temporary glitch. And the Jersey shore's not going anywhere soon."

"Not unless you count the sand eroding away," I said.

"Smart aleck."

Dad pulled the van onto a gravel lane.

"What are you doing?" I asked.

"I saw a sign for a farm stand," he said, and then there it was. "I thought it might be fun."

We pulled into the stand's small parking area and got out of the vehicle.

"What about your hat?" Dad asked.

"How can anybody from the Core know we're here?" I asked.

He shrugged. "Put it on."

I yanked it onto my head, and then we approached the stand.

One of the people working there was a girl about my age, a girl with rippling long black hair. Hanna, people called her.

"Hanna, can you get me some of those—"

"Hanna, can you get me some of these other—"

"Hanna, do you have any—"

"Busy spot," I said to Dad. I looked around. "What do you want to buy? We don't even have a kitchen."

Then I saw someone eating a cookie. It looked so good!

"Oh, cookies, Dad. Let's buy some."

"You'll never taste better." The man who spoke had a voice with sort of a twang to it.

"Get 'em while they're hot." Hanna's voice had it too. "Fresh out of the oven."

So we went up to the counter where she was standing.

"Sugar or chocolate chip?" Hanna asked. "Pretty hair."

I reached up to find an escaping tendril and pushed it to safety. "Thanks. Yours is pretty too." I looked up at my father. He shrugged at me. Probably okay. Don't worry. "Sugar cookies, Dad?" They were Mom's favorite.

"Half a dozen sugar cookies, miss," he said to Hanna.

She smiled and exchanged a warm bag filled with the goodies for Dad's payment, and then we walked back to the car. Boy, those cookies smelled wonderful! We opened the bag and took our first bites before we even got to the Caravan.

"Perfect!" proclaimed Dad. "Puts a perfect cap on the day."

Those cookies disappeared into our stomachs while farm after farm zoomed past my window. By the time the cookies—all except one—were gone, we were back in the city, with its sidewalks and stores and apartment complexes everywhere we looked.

Farther and farther into the city, and then, after a slow, slow turn, we were back at the Blue Moon.

Oh.

The hotel.

We got out of the van and entered the lobby. Everything was made real again. Going to the museum, looking at the Kansas landscape, buying cookies at the farm stand, that was all unreal, pretend stuff. If you don't count the out-of-body experience with the Gary Carmichael look-alike, all that could have been something I was doing with just my dad on an ordinary day we both had off from school but Mom didn't.

Well, it *was* something I had done with just my dad, but with the feeling of before, when we could still go home at the end of the day. That was the problem. We couldn't.

Once, he and I had gone to the Poconos when Mom had had to attend a three-day teachers' conference. That trip was so great—smelling the crisp autumn air, tramping along puddly dirt paths, coming upon a sunlit creek with orangey leaves floating in it. That was the best part, just coming upon that.

On the way home we'd stopped at a bakery and bought some cookies for Mom, except we ate all of them on the way back without realizing it. They were so good! I knew we'd eaten some, but I didn't think we'd eaten them all. Certainly there had to be two left.

Mom had run down the steps when she'd heard us come in, all smiles, like we were the best thing she'd ever seen.

"We brought you some cookies, Mom," I'd said after the hugs, and I'd handed her the bag.

She'd looked inside it and said, "Did I do something wrong?" because all that was left was crumbs.

"Oh, Dad!" I'd smacked my forehead with the heel of my hand. "How stupid! We ate 'em all."

Mom'd laughed and laughed, and I'd almost been glad we'd been so stupid like that because she'd laughed so hard. We'd joined in with her, but I think we'd both felt really dumb. "So I guess you guys aren't hungry," she'd said. "We'll have dinner tomorrow."

So after that, whenever Dad and I came back from one of those trips, and sometimes just when Dad picked me up at Jackie's, we'd come back and Mom would ask, "Bring me any cookies?"

So we always did, at least whenever Dad and I did anything like the Poconos trip or a day in New York for a rehearsal of one of his shows.

It had felt right to buy the cookies at the farm stand, had felt like the right, high-spirited thing to do. But now we were back at the hotel and reality with one cookie left, one we couldn't eat because it was Mom's, and no more pretending. We weren't home, Mom wasn't going to run down the steps, she wasn't going to smile at us like we were the greatest thing since sliced bread and ask, "Did you bring me any cookies?"

The hotel.

The hotel with its oppressive green velvet couches in the lobby, and pictures of silos on the walls.

"The hotel's all right," I told Dad. My legs felt heavy as we walked on to our suite. "It's just—I don't know. I don't want to be here. I want to go home. I feel like things would be better if we could just go home." We entered the suite, and I put the almost-empty bag on the coffee table.

Dad dropped the van keys next to the bag. "I feel the same way, but you know what? It's a feeling, and that's all it is. It wouldn't be better. Mom would still not be there, and we wouldn't be safe. Before anything else, that's what we need to be. We can't lose sight of that."

"But we're away from everything Mom ever did. Maybe the house still smells like her. We could go back there and be able to smell her even if she's not there." *If? If?* I didn't want to listen to reality. Make it go away. Make it and its goopy, sewery smell go away.

"We could." Dad nodded. "Still. Safer here." He opened the bag and took out the remaining cookie. I didn't want him to do that. He broke it in half and gave me one of the pieces. I didn't want him to do that, either. "To Mom and safety," he said, tapping my half of the cookie with his, like it was a champagne toast.

I knew Mom wasn't going to eat the cookie, but if *we* ate it, she sure couldn't. We should be saving it, putting it in a drawer with her name on it for when things . . . well, when she . . . my thought deteriorated and fell apart. What was the end of that sentence? Even I couldn't pretend hard enough and long enough to get there.

"Come on," said Dad, like he knew what I was feeling. Maybe he did.

"All right," I said, and gave his half-cookie a tap back. "To Mom and safety."

Dad ate his half, and I ate mine, even the crumbs.

Were we safer here? Maybe. Safer, but stuck on a bridge. That was what it felt like—a bridge that had the center slashed away. Twenty feet of space between me and where my next step had to fall. And underneath, a running, raging ocean of a river. Impossible to swim across, impossible to jump over. But that was what we had to do.

Chapter 11

The cell phone rang.

"Hello? . . . Yes, good morning, Mr. Swensen." Of course. Who else? He was the only one with the number. "Yes. . . . Really?" Dad smiled at me over his breakfast coffee the next morning while he listened. "All right. Two o'clock? Sure. Fine. See you then." He put the phone away.

"Did they catch him?" I asked. "Is it time to go back East and finish with all this?"

"Oh, no, nothing like that," said Dad.

Then, who cared? I slouched back in the booth and glanced around at the other diners. Eating, talking. Normal stuff. *Don't you get it?* I wanted to shout at them. *Don't you get it?* What didn't they get? That I couldn't go home?

"Mr. Swensen found us a house," Dad said. "No more hotel living."

I sat up. "Oh." I did care. "How'd he find us a house? Whose is it? Have they used it for witnesses before?"

"Well, I think he was purposely vague on that point, but I don't think any witnesses were ever hidden in this house before. There's some kind of trusted connection that lets us use this house, but it's probably not a good idea for Mr. Swensen to tell us more than that."

I raised my eyebrows at Dad. "Do you think it's all right? Do you think we'll be safe there? We don't know this connection. It could be—"

"We have to trust Mr. Swensen to do his job."

"But—"

"The marshals have protected us so far, haven't they? They know how to do this."

I nodded. "All right." I bounced a little in my booth and tried to look perky. "I am now officially enthusiastic."

Dad smiled. "That's my girl."

"So where's the house?"

"It's about forty miles away," he said, "on a farm."

"A farm? Oh, wow! A farm!" I was now more than officially enthusiastic. "We get to live on a farm?"

Dad laughed. "It's not the main house, but a little one next to where the farmer lives."

"But a farm!" I bounced some more. "Well, where is it? When can we go? I'm ready."

Dad smiled. "Imagine living with roosters or ducks or sheep. Maybe cows or horses."

"Jackie would laugh," I said. "Maybe . . . maybe she could come visit if we're there long enough. It would be fun."

"Sure. Maybe we'll work the land right along with the farmers. Maybe we'll love it so much, we'll stay after the trial and buy our own farm. Jackie could visit and hoe beans in rhythm with us."

"While we sing 'I've Been Working on the Railroad,'" I added.

"Sure," Dad said. "You can't hoe beans without a good work song."

I laughed. "When do we go?"

"We're meeting Mr. Swensen at the hotel at two o'clock. He'll take us."

"Today? That fast?"

"So he says."

"Well, Dad," I said, "maybe we should hurry. We have so much to pack."

He grinned at me. "Very funny. But we do have a little shopping to do so we can have sheets and towels for the new place. Get some groceries. Things like that. We're not going to be near stores, I'm betting."

We didn't exactly hurry. We took our time finishing breakfast, for instance, but we didn't hang around afterward for Dad to have his usual second cup of coffee. He took it to go, and we went to one of the malls, where we bought what food and linens we needed. Afterward we returned to the hotel and packed everything up. Then we took one last swim in the Blue Moon's pool.

"Not bad having a pool we can swim in every day." I pushed off one side and floated. "I don't suppose the farm has that."

"Doubt it." Dad stretched his arms out over the edge of the pool, the water lapping his chin. "I think Mr. Swensen would have said so."

"I'd still rather live in a house than a hotel." I pushed off the opposite side and floated again. "Even if it doesn't have a pool."

"That's an awful lot like what we've always done," said Dad.

"Then, I guess it will feel like home."

After a while we got out of the water, dried off, and sat at one of the poolside tables to eat the sandwiches we'd bought at the supermarket, me in that big bucket hat so I could take off the bathing cap. Somebody *could* show up.

When the sandwiches were gone, Dad stretched and said, "Well, little one?"

Back to the suite for showers and the final packing. By two o'clock we were ready and waiting in the parking lot for Mr. Swensen. A minute after two o'clock he pulled up next to us in the red Subaru. I looked around. Nobody watching. So what if it was the red Subaru from our trip from the airport? There had to be millions of those.

"All set?" Mr. Swensen asked.

Dad opened the driver side door of the van. "All set," he answered.

I gave the Blue Moon one last look before getting into the passenger side. A concrete place with blue script letters on the front. It hadn't been a bad place to stay, not really. We'd been safe there, and I'd felt the warmth of its protecting walls, but still I was glad to leave.

After all—a house on a farm! That was pretty exciting. And maybe Jackie *could* come out to see us. Sometime. I pictured a clapboard house with some interesting little additions and hidden stairways that generation after generation had added on. A tire swing in the back, and fields and fields of sunflowers in all directions, like some pictures I'd seen of France! A house on a farm! Cool!

We followed Mr. Swensen's car, heading out the way Dad and I had gone when we'd ended up at the museum. After a while we found ourselves approaching the sign for the farm stand we'd visited the day before.

"Maybe we'll get to eat more of those cookies," I said to Dad.

He grinned. "Some compensation."

And then Mr. Swensen turned his car into the lane where the sign pointed.

"Well!" said Dad. "Can you believe it?"

We passed the farm stand, which looked empty and forlorn, and then suddenly there we were. Two houses, one with three stories, one with two. Ours had to be the smaller boxy one with oatmeal-colored siding.

I didn't like the house. In fact I hated it. It was so flat, like someone had taken a fist and squashed the roof into itself. It was bad enough that the land was so flat, but somehow the house being so flat and so square too made everything just horrible. Not even a tree. No rosebushes by the front door or anything.

The small front porch looked about two inches deep, hardly room for the two chairs folded up against the house, with their backs to us. Before I even had a *chance* to hate the chairs, the chairs hated me.

"Great."

"Give it a chance." Dad opened his door, and the heat from the fields—no sunflowers, either—immediately hit me in the face and knocked out the air-conditioning that had made the afternoon bearable. It was even worse than the day before.

"Who can breathe this?" I asked.

"We can," said Dad.

Mr. Swensen was already out of his car, greeting a man wearing jeans, a T-shirt, and boots. A big straw hat.

"That will be the farmer." Dad leaned over and stepped out, unfolding his long body until I could see only as far up as his ribs. He bent back down to look at me. "You get out too." So I did. Whatever. Dad and I left the van and joined the marshal. But what for? This house stank. I might as well have stayed in the van while Dad said no. We would only be here about a minute.

Mr. Swensen introduced us to the farmer. "Mr. Weston and Linda. Mr. Jones." I had to remember which one of us was which. Who was Mr. Jones? Who was Mr. Weston? *I'm Linda, I'm Linda.*

I hung back, but Dad shook hands with Mr. Jones while the marshal kept on talking. He acted like he was some kind of liaison for a business Dad worked for, and Dad and I went along with him. Witness protection program meant secret, right? We couldn't actually tell the truth.

We're here in the witness protection program.

Oh, really? What did you do?

I don't know, but someone wants to kill me.

Then, forget it. We don't want dead bodies cluttering up the landscape.

Or—

We're in the witness protection program.

(Farmer contacts Carmichael. We're dead in twenty-four hours. The end.)

Skipping the truth was a much better idea.

"We can move right in, I understand," said Dad.

"If you like the place," said the farmer. "It would be good to see someone in here." He paused. "The house has been empty a long time."

Mr. Jones waited outside while Dad and I followed Mr. Swensen into the house, which was just a little cooler than the murderous outdoors. "The air conditioner's only been on a few minutes," Mr. Swensen explained.

I hated everything about the place—the clumpy stairs of dark wood, the green-flowered wallpaper in the dining room, the green-painted baseboard that edged all the walls. What was with all the green?

I particularly hated the stain in the bathroom sink, all brown over the cracked porcelain. I hated everything about the house, but I said nothing while Mr. Swensen took us from room to room to room.

Not here. Not here. Don't make us stay here.

"Nice and quiet," Mr. Swensen said. "You shouldn't have any trouble at all. And you're close to Wichita. When Linda has to go back to testify—"

No.

I dropped behind and stayed in the back bedroom he'd circled us through, and I closed the door behind them. *There. And stay away.*

There would be no trial. They'd never find that guy Carmichael, and I wouldn't have to testify and get shot by one of his henchmen when I went to the witness stand. At least the bad guys wouldn't find me here.

I hoped nobody would find me here, including me.

I glanced around the musty room with its wood-paneled walls and a closet you could almost not see except for the hook-and-eye closure that made it different from what surrounded it. A couple of nails in the wall where pictures had hung. This wasn't going to be *my* bedroom, I knew that. Well, of course not. We weren't going to stay here, so it couldn't be my bedroom. We *couldn't* stay *here*.

The muffled conversation between Dad and Mr. Swensen made it a little too well through the walls, so I hummed to block out their voices.

Oh, Eliza, little Liza Jane. Oh, Eliza, little Liza Jane!

The humming could cover their voices, but it couldn't mask what the cobwebby window showed me: flat, flat, and more flat.

Where were all the people? Hiding in the corn? Who was going to eat all that corn? Was it as good as the corn in Pennsylvania? No. No place this flat could grow good corn the way Pennsylvania could.

All right, Liza, get a grip. There are places in Pennsylvania that look this empty. Maybe not this flat, but this empty. You've just never been there. And why shouldn't Kansas grow corn that tastes good? They know how to farm here. Does corn really know a hill from level ground?

"Liza."

I whirled around. Dad was coming into the room, an anxious look on his face. Beyond him Mr. Swensen clumped away from us down the wooden stairs. We listened as the marshal reached the bottom and opened the front door.

"Well, sir . . . ," he began, and then the door closed, leaving the house silent. I stared at Dad.

"I know, I know," he said. "It's awful."

"So we don't have to stay?"

"Oh, we have to stay. We don't have much choice about that."

"But, Dad. We didn't do anything wrong. Why do we have to stay in a place like this like we're being punished? Why do they get to tell us where we have to live? We're not the bad guys."

"Well, we could be uncooperative," said Dad. "But don't we want to be alive?"

I sighed and frowned and paced. Jackie was never coming here. Not as long as Dad asked questions like that. How could I forget and think she could?

"It's just temporary," said Dad. "We're not going to stay forever. I promise. But for now we'll manage."

"I hate it here," I said. "It's disgusting."

"I know," he said. "It's not home."

"It sure isn't. I bet they've never even heard of rosebushes here."

"Maybe not, but this is our only option right now. Later we can find somewhere else. Someplace we like better."

"How about home?"

"Could be," said Dad, "this whole thing will blow over real soon. We may very well be back in time for school. Who knows? Maybe our house won't even be sold by then, and we can move right back in."

I shrugged my shoulders. Going home just didn't feel likely.

"Try," said Dad. "Please?"

It wasn't his fault. I turned a smile on him. "Okay." And the anxious look on his face relaxed some.

"That's my girl."

We went back downstairs and returned to the porch and the unbreathable air, where Dad said, "Perfect. We'll stay."

Yeah, right. What about that sink? What about the cobwebs?

The flat roof? What about that hook and eye? But I didn't say anything. We weren't staying. Not for long.

Perfect? Who'd believe that?

"Excellent!" Mr. Jones looked at us curiously, but he said no more. He must have thought it was weird that we would just show up and move in, especially since the house was so awful. He must have known we were running from someone if we were so anxious to dig in after hardly looking at the place. Who would want to stay here?

We're the good guys, I wanted to tell him, but how could I say that without saying that there were bad guys? That we were in danger, and that if the Core knew where we were, there'd be blood and dead bodies right here on this porch. *So we can't tell you, since you might know someone who happens to know someone who happens to know Gary Carmichael.*

Stupid. It was all stupid. Just not stupid enough.

"Good!" Mr. Swensen shook hands with everybody again, then disappeared out the gravel drive in his Subaru, and the place was ours.

Who signed the lease or how it was done, I never found out. Hocus-pocus-abracadabra: You're a Kansas farm girl, and your name is Linda. *Poof!*

Chapter 12

I watched Mr. Swensen's car disappear behind some cornstalks, and then I turned toward Dad. I wanted to say something about this place where we were stuck, about how I hoped we wouldn't be there long, but I couldn't with Mr. Jones still there. I gave him the best smile I could force, but it didn't feel real great. Couldn't we just go inside? Wasn't the place ours now?

"Beautiful spot," said Dad.

"Yeah," I said, and my smile felt even more forced. I guessed it was beautiful. If you like flat houses and million-degree heat.

But Mr. Jones smiled, apparently happy that we liked where we were.

"Welcome to Jones's Paradise." He made a large gesture. "My pride and joy."

"I can see why," said Dad.

I turned to look around. A girl with her head buried in a book sat maybe a hundred feet away on the wooden fence that bordered the field. I hadn't noticed her before.

"I understand you'll be working from here, Mr. Weston."

"Call me Harve," said Dad. *Harve?* Well, same as I was Linda. "This seems like a good quiet place."

"One thing about this area," said Mr. Jones, "is the quiet. Sometimes it's so quiet, the quiet makes a noise of its own and wakes us up at night. When it's *real* quiet, it wakes the dead, and we hear the rattling of their chains."

"What?" I didn't mean to say anything, but that was so weird.

"You'll see," said Mr. Jones.

I looked at Dad, and he winked at me. Oh. A joke. I smiled.

"So, Linda," Mr. Jones said to me, "do you know how to ride a horse?"

"No."

"Talk to my daughter about it. She'll teach you. She thinks everybody should ride."

"Horseback riding lessons?" I looked at Dad again.

"We could look into it," he said. "When in Rome, you know."

"There's Hanna now." Mr. Jones pointed to the girl on the fence. "Talk to her while your dad and I discuss a few things. She won't mind putting that book down."

"Hanna?" I asked. "The girl who sold us cookies yesterday?"

"Oh, you've been here already," said Mr. Jones. "A sneak preview."

"Sort of by accident," said Dad. "We were just driving around."

"Well, a lucky accident," said Mr. Jones. "Lucky for you if you got some of my wife's cookies. They go fast."

I stared at Hanna. She was still reading, a book in one hand and a red apple in the other. She hadn't eaten any of the apple that I could tell, and I wondered what book made her forget she even held it.

"Go see her," urged Mr. Jones. "Ask her to show you the horses. Ask her about riding lessons."

"But—" *The flashbacks*, my eyes said to Dad.

"I'll be right here," he said. "Either in the house or on the porch. Go ahead."

Ride? Ride a horse?

I didn't know what to say to *them*, but here's what I said to myself: *Sure. I'll learn to ride a horse. I'll learn to ride a tractor. I'll learn to ride a hot-air balloon. What difference does it make? Give me a kangaroo, and I'll ride it, too. Why not? I might as well, as long as I'm not living my life.*

Did it really matter what the filling-in stuff was that I'd do until my life showed up again? The stuff I'd do until my life's merry-go-round made a complete 360 to where I'd fallen off, and where I'd get back on it again, picking the gravel from the fall out of my knee and going back to what I knew?

Maybe that was it. This part of my life wasn't real. In fact, it wasn't even my life. Someone else was riding my bike in Avon, buying basketball shoes in Avon, and joking with Jackie in

Avon, while I got ready to take this other person's horse rides in a place that didn't look anything like any part of Pennsylvania. I wondered if Kansas was a real place. Truly. Could any place really, really be this flat and hot?

I wasn't asleep and dreaming. I knew it. But I kind of believed I was. Otherwise, how could any of this make sense?

Maybe by the time I woke up from this nightmare, I'd at least have done something. Learned to ride a horse. Maybe I'd like knowing how to do that when I was Liza Wellington again. Sure. Wake up from a nightmare and—Hey! Presto! I can play the piano!

"Hanna can at least show you the horses," said Mr. Jones. "You don't have to actually get on one if you don't want."

I still hesitated.

"Hanna's friendly," said Mr. Jones. "You'll like her."

So I walked across the driveway to the fence directly opposite, before turning around to look back at Dad. Still there, still there. He wasn't going anywhere, and I could still see him. Robert Bramwell's ghost couldn't do much to me as long as I could see Dad. I continued on, only now I walked backward along the fence, backward, backward, keeping my eye on Dad. Until I hit something.

"Hey!" Hanna's foot.

"Oh, sorry." A quick glance at Hanna, then one last look at Dad before I pretended I didn't need to keep looking at him.

Hanna stared up at me. Even on the fence, she was shorter than I was, and her black hair showed blue highlights in the sun where it escaped from her hat. Thick black lashes outlined a pair of wide blue eyes. *How do you get lashes that thick?*

"I'm Linda." *Linda. Linda Weston.* "My dad and I are moving in over there." *Lindalindalinda.*

"Hey, Linda," she said. "Welcome to Jones's Paradise." She cocked her head. "I remember you from the stand. How were the cookies?"

"Great."

She splayed her book over the fence and jumped down. I glanced at the title. *Great Expectations.* The opposite of my life: *No Expectations* or *Lost Expectations* or *Expectations?—Huh! Don't Make Me Laugh!*

"Good book?

"I'm reading it for school," she told me.

"Do you like it?"

"It's pretty good." She stuck the apple into her hip pocket. Maybe she just didn't feel like eating it, and not eating it had nothing to do with the book. I noticed the other hip pocket had its own bulge. Two pockets, two apples. Maybe she just liked to be balanced. "You have to concentrate, though. Did Dad tell you about the horses?"

"As a matter of fact," I said, "he did. But I don't know how to ride."

"You *have* to learn how to ride," she said. "It's the best." She ducked underneath the top fence rail and stood looking at me from the other side. "Come on. We'll get you up on Peaches."

Peaches? But—but—I didn't want to get up onto a horse. I was just coming to look.

"Come on." Hanna pointed at a building. "She's on the other side of the stable."

I ducked between the fence rails too and followed her across the field. So big, so wide, so flat, and *so hot*!

"How do you breathe this air?" I asked.

"It's hot even for us," said Hanna, "but you'll get used to it." She grinned at me. "You're from the East, right?"

"How do you know? Because I can't breathe this air?"

"That and your accent."

"Oh." I thought of her mild twang. "I guess I don't sound like I'm from here."

"Nope. You don't. Where are you from?"

Where was I from? Oh, yeah.

"New Jersey," I said. "A little town in south Jersey."

We talked a little more about accents and hot air and anything else I could grab hold of, and suddenly around the corner of the stable was the biggest, brownest horse I ever saw.

I backed away. I wasn't so sure I liked being this close. Maybe I didn't like horses. They were better in pictures. They couldn't bite you, anyhow, from the pages of a magazine or a scrapbook.

Hanna was between me and the horse, but that horse was way bigger than Hanna. I looked back to where Hanna's book still lay, so far away and small. Dad's head appeared beyond it over the fence. If I ran, would the horse run after me? I'd never make it. I'd get about three steps before the horse knocked me down. Not as scary as Robert Bramwell, but scary enough.

But Hanna—she didn't act scared or anything.

"Meet Peaches." Peaches stopped nibbling to extend a long muzzle to my new friend. Hanna pulled out the apple from her left hip pocket and offered it to the horse. *Munch, munch, munch.* Oh, that's why Hanna hadn't eaten it. It was for the horse. "She's a mare."

Mer, French for "sea." *La mer:* the sea. Visions of Sea Isle City and saltwater taffy washed over me.

Mare. Mer. Sea. "La Mer" was the name of a piece of music Dad liked. *Stop! Stop-stop!*

"A girl horse," added Hanna.

Mares eat oats and does eat oats—

Stop!

I spoke over my faster and faster thoughts. "Oh. I knew that. A mare. *Mare.*" As in "mother horse." French for "mother." "*La mère*" equals "the mother." "*Ma mère*" means "my mother." *Ma mère est dans la mer.* My mother is in the sea. No, she isn't. *Ma mère est*—My mother is—My mother is—

Not now!

I swallowed and concentrated hard on the horse. So far off the ground! And her eyes? How big! Anything with eyes that big, I wasn't sure I wanted to get near.

"I don't know." What was I doing here? I backed up some more. "Maybe this isn't such a good idea." Another couple of steps. Peaches hadn't moved. Another step. "I've never been on a horse in my life. I play basketball, and I like to read, but I've never been on a horse."

Can horses smell fear? Can Gary Carmichael? *Stop it!*

"Who's your favorite author?" Hanna asked.

"Oh, I love everybody," I said, but still I watched the horse. It—she—didn't care if I read anything ever. I wasn't sure she cared about me, period, which would have been just fine if only I could have been sure about that. "Lisa Scottoline," I blathered on. "Toni Morrison. Stephen King."

"I like them too," said Hanna. She took my hand and pulled me forward so she could place it on Peaches's side. Warm. Under Hanna's fingers I stroked Peaches. Peaches turned her head to look at me. I bit my lip, but that was all Peaches did. Looked at me, then turned her head away as if to say *You bore me.*

"Nice," I said, but I sure wasn't getting up on her.

Hanna didn't ask me to. She could tell, for sure, how I felt.

"Wait a sec!" Hanna ran inside the stable and came out again with a couple of combs. "Here." She handed me one. "Do what I do."

We combed and combed while we talked about stuff we'd read. Mostly Hanna asked questions and I answered. Once in a while Peaches would look back at us, move her feet, wiggle her ears. Once, she whinnied.

"A real horse," I remarked when she did that.

"We don't go for the fake kind around here. Okay." Hanna took the comb away from me. "Enough with the comb." She removed the apple from her right hip pocket and presented it to me. "Reward time." I looked at her like she was crazy. Dirty horsey hands handing me an apple?

"I'm not hungry," I said, "but thanks." I tried to give it back. This was how you rewarded people in Kansas? By giving them disgusting apples?

"Not *your* reward," she said. "It's for Peaches, silly."

"Peaches?" I looked from the apple to Hanna. "Then, why give it to me?"

"So *you* can give it to her. So she can know you a little bit better. And vice versa."

I looked at Peaches's mouth and then at Hanna.

"Go ahead," she said. "She won't bite."

"Are you sure?"

"I've never known Peaches to bite anyone. I swear. She's gentle."

Then I guess Peaches got tired of the whole thing, because— *Snatch!* She just went for it. Her lips met my hand, and the apple was hers.

Wet! Wet! Ugh! I jumped backward and fell down hard on my butt. On impact my hat fell onto the ground. Oh, well. Hanna knew I was a redhead from our visit to the farm stand. No secrets there. I wiped my hand on my jeans and shivered. *Ugh!*

Hanna laughed. "You okay there?" She reached her hand to mine and helped me to my feet. "All right?" She leaned over and picked up my hat.

"Except for the feeling stupid part." I shivered again. At least Peaches hadn't bitten me. But that mouth!

"Feeling stupid isn't fatal," said Hanna.

"I guess it's better than actually being stupid," I said.

"There you go."

I brushed off my rear before we set off away from Peaches. With each step I felt more comfortable. I did look back once in a while to see where she was. Always where we'd left her, not even looking at us, not caring. I guessed she figured no more apples were forthcoming and we were boring. "Forthcoming." What kind of a word was that? A Linda word, not a Liza word. "Forthcoming." Right. Jackie would laugh at me for thinking it.

I was still nervous. The sooner we put our bodies on the other side of the fence, the better I'd like it. Peaches could still decide we weren't boring. I twisted my torso to pretend to check my rear for dried grass or dirt, but I was really checking on Peaches. Still there. I brushed off my rear again for what I pretended I'd missed the last time.

"Good job." Hanna twirled my hat on her fingers. "Maybe we'll get you up on her tomorrow."

"Okay. I'll try."

"And then we can play a little basketball, if you want. There's an old hoop over by the barn." The hat twirled off her hand before she caught it with her other one and stuck it onto her head, covering the hat already there.

I grinned. "That's the reward for me, I guess, huh?"

"Hey, why not? The ol' carrot on the stick."

"What, no apples?"

"Nope. Peaches ate 'em all."

We reached the fence and started between the rails.

"Ouch!" Some strands of my hair managed to catch in the rough wood. "Owww!"

"You have to watch out for these fences," said Hanna. "They bite."

"Here I was worried about the horse," I said, "and it turns out it's the fence that's dangerous." *Yank!* and I freed the strands.

Hanna laughed. "I like your sense of humor," she said. "Here." She reached her hands around my arm and helped me the rest of the way through, while I was careful to keep my head away from another entrapment.

As I emerged on the other side, a white station wagon filled with people crunched down the driveway and stopped in front of Hanna's house. Three other cars came in behind it, stopping too, and all the people in all four cars got out.

"What's going on?" More cars pulled up. Butterflies beat against my ribs. Was I safe? Was one of those people Gary Carmichael? Was I trapped? I needed my hat! Where was my hat? Hanna still had it on her head.

"Just customers," said Hanna with a shrug. "We always get them this time of day."

"What are you selling?" I asked her. "Could I have my hat?"

"Raw milk," she answered. With her eye on the newcomers she tugged on the hat, but it had clung to the one underneath it. She took both off together and worked her fingers between the rims.

"Raw milk?" How had the hats gotten so stuck together?

"It's good stuff. We test it all the time. I'll bring you some if there's any left."

"You know these people?"

She stopped with the hats to give me a puzzled look. "Of course." She turned toward the crowd. "Hey, Jackson, Trevor!" she called. "Hey, Maura!" And then she was introducing me to what felt like hundreds of people, gesturing with our hats as she did so. "Meet Linda."

Oh, well. Forget the hat now. Anyone who hadn't seen the color of my hair by this time was blind. Probably it didn't matter, anyway. Gary Carmichael here? Right.

"Hello," I said. "How do you do? Nice to meet you." Over and over, over and over.

"You're from the East," one of them said. A lady named Tonette. "I can tell by your accent. What brings you here?"

"Dad's work." I didn't want to tell them about Mom dying, which, anyway, wasn't the real reason we moved. "He wants quiet."

Tonette laughed. "Well, quiet is what you'll get."

"Hey, you look like that girl on TV," somebody said. A man with a gray ponytail.

Oh, no! "Well, I've never been on TV."

Hanna looked at me. "I was trying to think who you reminded me of."

"Someone on *American Idol*?" I said, because I had to keep pretending. "Not me. I can't sing at all." That news program aired weeks ago. They remembered it?

"Oh, no, it was a news story about some girl that's missing or run away," said the man with the ponytail. "I forget which. But she's a redhead. Looks just like you."

Help! Help! Help!

"She doesn't look like that girl at all," said Tonette. "They were talking about her on the recap last night, so I saw her picture. That girl's got a crooked nose and braces." Thank goodness for Tonette and her mistaken observation! But last night? Not just the one airing? But only the recap. Maybe just a montage of the month's stories. Probably.

"Hanna," shouted someone close to her house, "what about some milk?"

"Sure thing," said Hanna. The crowd eased toward Hanna's house, and she looked at me. "See you later, Linda. Welcome to the farm."

"Thanks."

I started to run. So what if somebody saw me run? Girls run. And, boy, I'd been wanting to *run!*

"Hey! Your hat!"

"Oh." I felt silly. The all-important hat, and here I was forgetting about it.

I took the hat, finally separated from Hanna's, and then we set off in opposite directions, me going to my house, my new home, while Hanna followed the milk customers to hers.

Dad was at the dining room table with his computer.

"It's cooler in here." I looked around the room. I liked the wallpaper better now, and the green woodwork didn't seem so bad. I still held a grudge against the stain in the sink upstairs, but the dining room I liked better.

"The air conditioner does a good job," said Dad. "How was Hanna? Did you have fun?"

"Sure," I said, "but I smell like a horse." I told him about combing Peaches and how Hanna liked to read too, and how all those people came to Jones's Paradise to buy raw milk. "Hanna said she'd bring us some if there was any left." I didn't tell how everybody'd seen my red hair and wondered if I was the girl on TV. Why worry him? And besides, it had ended okay. I didn't wear braces.

"Adventures all over," said Dad.

"The next one involves getting clean."

"Towels and clothes up in the hall," he informed me, and I headed for the steps.

Combing Peaches and talking with Hanna was fun, and for a few minutes I'd almost forgotten how things really were. But maybe, I thought as the shower rinsed off the sweat and horse stink, this was how getting through a disaster was done. Just by doing stuff—maybe it didn't matter what—and making friends. Not sitting around.

I spent some time after that unpacking, putting clothes in drawers, making my bed with the sheets we'd just bought. And when I slept that night with the warm Kansas air breezing through the room, I slept well.

Chapter 13

"Oh, Dad, look." The rays of the next afternoon's sun brightened the books I held aloft in the dining room. "The books we took out from the library."

Dad stopped typing to glance at them. "Oh, man. Where were they?"

"In this bag under your Phillies hat." I put on the hat and grinned at him from underneath the bill.

He grinned back, shaking his head. "I guess we couldn't remember everything. Feel like a trip back into town?"

I shrugged. "I don't know. I have so many appointments and so many people to see, I don't know if I can get away."

Dad threw a crumpled-up piece of paper at me. I caught it and threw it back at him. He dodged it, and the missile hit the floor by the window. "Okay," he said. He punched a few keys on his keyboard, closed the laptop in its case, and stood up. "Let's go."

"Right now? Back to Wichita?"

"Yeah. Otherwise we might forget again. Then the library police will be after us."

"Better them than some other people," I said.

"Have you *met* the library police?"

Laughing, I tossed Dad his hat, and grabbed mine. Then we headed for the door. He carried his computer with him.

"Why are you bringing that?" I asked.

"I might do a little work at the library," he answered. "You don't care, do you?"

"I guess not. I suppose I should plan to read while we're there."

"Well, I understand they've got books handy," Dad said.

I made a face at him as we left the house, and we were laughing when we heard the crunch of gravel. Hanna was walking toward us.

"Nice day, isn't it?" She hefted a box in her arms. "I'm sorry," she said. "We sold out the raw milk yesterday."

"Whatcha got there?" I asked.

"Sugar cookies for the stand." Her eyes went from Dad to me. "Two hats with those *P*s. What team is that?"

"Oh!" I touched my hat and looked at Dad's. "We're from Phillies country."

I wondered if that was saying too much, giving too much away, but Hanna—what was she going to do? Tell someone she knew some Phillies fans? There were only about three zillion of us. Probably more than us two, even, in the state of Kansas. After all, it was in Kansas where we'd bought the hats. Somebody besides us must have been buying them.

"I thought you said you were from New Jersey."

"We are," said Dad, and I could feel him shift gears to jump with the conversation. "Half of New Jersey roots for the Phillies. The other half—well, they're misguided."

"Ah." Hanna shifted the box. "Well, you have a good day, Phillies fans. I have to get up to the stand."

Whew! Got out of that one!

"Tell you what, Hanna," said Dad. "We'll drive you to the stand, and then we'll relieve you of some of those cookies."

"Oh, why don't we relieve her of *all* the cookies?" I asked. "Then you won't have to go to the stand at all, right, and—even better—we'll have cookies."

She laughed. "You want eight dozen cookies?"

"Maybe a dozen," said Dad.

"Deal. For the car ride."

"Hey," I said, "*I* might want eight dozen cookies."

Hanna looked at me with a pseudo-grown-up raised-eyebrow look. "The limit, young lady, is two cookies."

"Aww."

Hanna laughed again. "I have to go up anyway," she said. "There's lots of stuff to sell besides these cookies."

She took a seat in the back of the van and put the box on the spot beside her. I took my place on the other side of the box. The cookies filled the air with such an aroma!

"Oh, man, sugar cookies," I said. "Mmm." I could almost taste them.

"They won't last," said Hanna.

"With good reason," said Dad.

We drove about fifteen seconds before we pulled into the parking lot for the stand.

"Here she is," I heard someone say. "Here's the cookie lady."

Dad carried the box for Hanna into the structure, and Hanna grinned at me.

"Boy," she said, "such treatment. I'll be too spoiled to walk back later."

We followed Dad, and all those people followed us, jockeying for a position in line for what was in the box. "Hey, Hanna, do you have—"

"Hey, Hanna, I'm looking for—"

"Hanna!"

"Hanna!"

"Hanna!"

"Oh, to be so important," I said to her.

"It comes with the cookies," she said. "Without the cookies, they don't even know my name."

Dad bought the first dozen from Hanna, and then we returned to the parking area. I looked back from the van and waved at my new friend. Her hands were busy, but she gave me a grin.

We can live here. It will be okay.

Dad bit into a cookie and winked at me. Then we drove off.

By the time we reached the Wichita library, half the cookies were gone. Not more, because Dad said something about restraint and set the bag on the seat behind him.

I gave him a pretend pout, and he said, "They'll be good for the trip back."

"Yes, but will I?"

"Ha, ha."

We parked in the library lot and went inside. I dropped the books in the return slot and followed Dad, browsing through the shelves as I went.

"Oh." Dad stopped, and I ran into him. "Oh, sorry, babe."

"Is this the comedy number in your show?" I asked. "I missed the rehearsal."

"I'll write it in," said Dad. "Actually, I forgot the computer. It's still in the van."

I pivoted on the tile floor and headed for the exit. "I'll get it."

"Hold up," said Dad. "The van's locked." He started to give me the keys, then said, "No. I'll go for it if I find anything worthwhile in here. But first I want to look at some newspapers."

"I thought we weren't looking at newspapers," I said.

"I think we can handle it now. Besides, I want to see if we're going to have a strike at Temple. Probably not. The negotiations had been going well. But maybe there's a paper here that will say. Or I can check online on one of the library's computers."

"It's a pain not having Internet at the house," I said.

"Patience," said Dad. "We will."

We headed deeper into the library to where the magazines and newspapers were kept.

"Not a bad idea to get caught up on the world, anyway," Dad remarked. He put on his reading glasses and sat down with a copy of the *New York Times* while I squatted down to browse through the nearby magazine rack. *Time*, the *Smithsonian*, *People*. What did I want? The *New Yorker*, *Farm and Home*? What? What I really wanted was something funny. I pushed back the rim of my hat so it wouldn't get between me and the titles I was trying to read.

I felt pretty good. I mean, I still felt sad about Mom and all that. That didn't go away, and the phantom Mr. Bramwell could surface anytime, but Dad and I—I was getting a glimmer that maybe we'd be okay. We could make it through this.

I picked up the latest *Newsweek* and stood again, glancing at Dad as I did. He turned a page of his newspaper, and his shoulder stiffened. Bad news from Temple? I pretended not to see his frown—there'd been enough bad news—and began fanning through the pages of my magazine. Maybe we'd go back to shunning newspapers. I didn't care.

I fanned through my magazine, not really looking at it, not really caring about it, just waiting for Dad. A splash of color—

What? Huh? Wait!

I pushed back the pages, looking for it again. It couldn't have been—no—I couldn't have seen—

No—

Yes.

My hair. *My* face.

"*What?*"

Dad was rising and coming close, a look in his eyes through those reading glasses that said he thought I was going to be sick or something.

Other people stared too. What was the matter with everybody? I was the one with the magazine. Nobody else was looking at it. Nobody else could know what I'd seen in it. Could they?

"What's the matter?" Dad asked.

I showed him the article. WHAT REALLY HAPPENED? BROADWAY COMPOSER AND DAUGHTER MISSING. That was the title. And there was a color shot of me, and then lots of words. Was my hair really that magenta?

Dad tapped his newspaper. "It's in here, too." He kept his voice low.

I kept my voice down, same as his. "In the *New York Times*?"

"I guess it wasn't just a one-shot deal on that television show." No. I should have told him what the milk buyers had said. But I'd thought— "People are reading about us all over the country. Some journalist has a reward out for us."

"Can they do that?" I bent over the magazine article. "Can people really put out rewards to find people in the witness protection program? Shouldn't that be illegal?" I read a little further in the magazine. "It even puts out my height and weight and the number of points I scored playing basketball last season. Why does anybody care about that? And how come they know how much I weigh? Who told them? *You* don't even know that."

"The *Times* says maybe we've been killed and there's been a cover-up. The reporter's trying to prove it." He reached over and turned to the magazine's next page, and we saw more pictures of our family. None were very good likenesses of Dad, but without a doubt the pictures of me were of me.

There was a big picture of Mom, too. *Mom!* My hands squeezed into fists, and I wanted to hit somebody. *Ohhh! Leave her alone!*

"Why would there be a cover-up?" I asked. "Who would want to cover it up?"

"The reporter has some theory or other. It doesn't matter."

He took the magazine from me and closed it, put it back on the rack. Returned the newspaper to its shelf. "We better go," he whispered. He slipped his glasses into his breast pocket. "Come on."

I glanced around again. People were still looking at me. I could tell by their expressions that they didn't yet know what it was that had them puzzled. One lady's eyes were narrowing and narrowing. Any second—

The brim of my hat. I yanked on it so it would cover my face, but all that did was make my hair spill out all over. I stuffed it back in as fast as I could. My hair was covered now, but what could I do about my height? And had anybody noticed the hair? Had I gotten it all? Would anyone care?

Someone was coming toward me. A lady with gray-brown eyes. She was smiling.

"Miss?"

Run!

Dad's hand was on my arm. "No," he whispered. He must have sensed that I was about to rocket off. "We don't want to draw attention."

"Miss?"

Oh, no. Oh, no.

"Miss, you dropped something." She bent down and picked up my ponytail holder. Oh.

"Thank you," I said, and took it, put it over my wrist. I guessed I'd knocked it out of my hair when I'd yanked on the hat rim. "Thanks." Only the ponytail holder. I felt like I'd had a reprieve.

We didn't run, but we didn't waste any time either, getting back outside and into the parking lot.

And my hat! My troublemaking hat!

A sudden gust blew it off when we were about halfway to the van, and it sailed back the way we'd come. I chased the hat and chased it. Sea Isle City all over again, and I thought of Maxwell.

"Hey," someone shouted. "Hey! You're that girl! Hey!"

I stopped where I was and stared around. There—there— there. Everywhere, people stared back at me, at Dad. My mouth was stuck open while my eyes went from face to face to face.

"You're the girl, you're the girl! Hey!"

"I saw her first!"

"I did!"

Click! Someone took a picture. Another picked up my hat. *Click!* Another picture.

Dad's hand tugged on mine. "Quick! Quick!"

"Hey! Don't you want your hat?"

But we were running, almost flying. I didn't remember opening the van door, but there I was inside, groping for my seat belt while Dad gunned the engine into reverse, squealing tires, out of the parking space. Then forward, forward, forward to the exit.

Thunk! What was that? A rock? Who'd throw a rock at us? Why? But we turned onto the street and kept going.

It was so hot in the van. Once we were clear of the parking lot, Dad opened the windows, clearing out the hot air, billowing my hair around my face. I didn't have another hat in the van, and even though we didn't pass more than a couple of cars after we left the city, I felt like everybody in the world was staring at me and my hair. Everybody could see me and know everything about me!

Dangerdangerdangerdanger danger.

Not until we were almost to Jones's Paradise did I calm down enough to even look at Dad. His knuckles were white.

Dangerdangerdangerdanger danger.

"This is unbelievable." It was only then that I remembered the ponytail holder on my wrist. I wound it around the flyaway hair, pulling it into a bun.

"You said it, Liza." Dad caught me messing with my hair. "Here," he said. He took off his hat and gave it to me. The hat was loose on my head, and the visor fell low over my eyes.

*Dangerdangerdangerdanger*danger.

How long? How long before Gary Carmichael found us?

We got to a stop sign not far from Jones's Paradise and had to wait for three cars to turn onto the road in front of us.

"Three cars?" I said to Dad. "Three cars at once around here?"

"Probably milk customers," said Dad. "Or the farm stand business."

We watched. A blue car with a woman inside. I recognized her as Tonette from the day before. A milk customer. A green car carrying four men. All strangers to me. And another green car. This one held two, and in the passenger seat was Gary Carmichael.

No question.

As his car made the turn, he looked straight at me! But he gave no reaction. Why not? Could he play it that cool?

"See him, Dad?" I said it without moving my lips. "See him?"

"I saw," was Dad's grim reply. We sat for a few seconds to see what he and the other man in his car would do. Nothing. They just kept going, getting smaller and smaller but not disappearing on the long, flat road that led to Jones's Paradise. Oh, but for a hilly Pennsylvania road to make you vanish!

Dad turned the car to the left.

"He looked at me," I said. "He saw me. Why didn't he recognize me?"

Dad gave me a glance. "I'm not sure I'd recognize you either, with that hat over your eyes."

"So we're still okay?"

"We're still okay," said Dad. "Still okay and darn lucky."

Dad pulled the phone out of his pocket and handed it to me. "Push speed dial one," he said.

I did as he said. After three rings I got an answer.

"Mr. Swensen?"

Then I told him.

"Hold on," he said. There was a pause of maybe a minute. Then he was back. "Someone's on the way."

"Well, whoever it is won't see us," I said. "We're going in the opposite direction."

"Don't come back until I tell you it's clear."

Dad heard that. "Tell him . . . ," he said, and his voice was loud enough that Mr. Swensen could hear what he said too. "Tell him we're not coming back."

"All right," said the marshal. "That's reasonable."

"I hope the Joneses will be all right," I said.

"We'll make sure," Mr. Swensen said. "Where are you going?"

"Wait a second." I took the phone away from my mouth. "Where are we going, Dad?"

"I don't know. Just tell him we're heading East. When we get somewhere, I'll call him. Then we'll figure out what's next."

I spoke into the phone again. "Mr. Swensen?"

"I heard," he said. "I'll wait to hear from you. Call if there is any trouble at all."

"Don't worry," I said.

I hung up the phone and looked at Dad. He glanced at me.

"All right?" he asked.

"I'm fine," I said. "How about you?"

"Still alive."

"That's the point," I said. "That's the whole point."

Chapter 14

Dad and I were sitting in a rest area snack bar maybe six hours later. I'd told him what the milk buyers had said about seeing me on TV a couple of days before.

"I'm sorry," I said. "I should have told you. I didn't think it mattered, and I didn't want to worry you."

"Anytime," said Dad, "you think something might worry me, it matters enough to tell me. I can handle worry better than some other things."

I nodded, but I felt lousy about it. "Could we have done anything different?"

"I don't know what. Maybe we could have called Mr. Swensen earlier, but what he was going to do about it, I don't know. Even though we were on TV—if they didn't actually say where we were—we should still have been okay."

"Except one of the milk buyers might have ratted us out."

"Anyone might have. At the hotel, another hotel, in another neighborhood."

"So we weren't safe anywhere," I said.

"No."

"Is everybody a spy?" I glanced around at the sparsely filled place. A woman with three small children, two old men playing cards, and a boy about fourteen years old sipping on a soda. "Maybe we should get back in the van so no one can see us."

"I think we're okay here," Dad said. "We'll leave when we feel like it. No rush."

Dad was drinking coffee and I was eating the last of the french fries from my dinner. Well, I was mostly pushing them around my plate. Stacking them like Lincoln Logs and then knocking them down again to start over.

"Interesting game you have going over there," commented Dad.

"I'm thinking of marketing it," I told him. *Stack, stack.* "Want to play?"

The phone rang, and Dad pulled it out of his pocket. "Hello." Then mostly he listened. "I see. . . . Uh-huh. Thanks. Okay." He hung up and looked at me. "They didn't find 'em."

"I didn't think they would." I pushed the french fry wall over. "What's next?" *Stack, stack, stack.*

"We'll just go on," said Dad, "same as we've been doing." He drained his mug of the last few drops before leaving it on the table. "Ready?" He dropped a few bills onto the table, and we went back to the van.

"Where to?" I asked.

"East. Just east."

We drove until Dad was too tired to drive, and then we stopped at the first motel with a vacancy sign and flopped into bed.

Then up and out the next morning and driving again, but not for long. At about ten o'clock Dad pulled the van into the parking lot of a bank we happened to be passing.

"I have an account here," he told me. "I'm going to withdraw some money so we don't have to charge anything, so no one can track us by how we spend."

"But can't we be traced by the withdrawal?"

"Sure, but we won't be hanging around here to be found. Trust me."

Normally—what was normal anymore?—I would have stayed in the car and listened to the radio, but not now. I went with him and watched his transaction with one of the tellers. In a minute we were back in the parking lot, and Dad had a thousand dollars in his hip pocket that hadn't been there before.

"Isn't that a lot of money to be carrying around?" I asked.

"Sure. But it's not very traceable. That's what matters to me right now."

Then we went to a phone store, and when we came back into the sunshine, Dad had one of those prepaid phones in his pocket.

"What's that about?" I asked.

He dropped the phone we already had onto the parking

lot asphalt and stamped on it, smashing it completely. Then he threw it into a trash can.

What is this? "Are you crazy? What are you doing?"

"I'm probably out of my mind," he said, "but I just don't want anybody to know where we are. If someone can track us by that phone, then I don't want it."

"But the FBI—"

"I don't care about the FBI anymore. I don't care about anybody anymore. Just us. We are taking care of us."

"But—"

"And that's it!"

I raised my eyes to him. "Are you all right?"

"No. Why should I be? But we're better off on our own. Trust me."

We went next to a store that sold home security devices and came out with a surveillance detector.

"How'd you know where to find this?" I asked Dad.

"I saw an ad on the bulletin board at the phone store," he told me. "If I hadn't seen that, we would have gone to a library and looked for places that sell these. Seeing the ad saved us time."

Before we drove one more foot, we knew the van was clean of tracking and listening devices. No bugs were giving us away to anybody.

"Do you really believe anybody is caring enough about us to bug our car?" I asked.

"Not too long ago," said Dad, "I wouldn't have believed any of this."

"Couldn't we have used the surveillance detector for the phone?"

He shrugged. "Probably. But someone could still have tracked that phone whenever we used it. Now no one knows what phone we have. Hey, look at this."

Dad leaned into the middle of the van and brought out a bag before opening it. It contained the cookies he had made off-limits on our way to the library. Cookies. Surveillance detectors, smashed phones, and—and cookies?

Dad took one and bit into it.

"Still good," he said. He held out the bag to me. "Have one."

"No, thanks." Cookies and fear somehow did not go together.

Dad held out his cookie. "Take a small bite. It will cheer you."

"But—"

"It's not about the cookie."

"All right." I took a bite to please him.

The sweet taste was a sudden oasis from the world of people who wanted us dead. Lots of people loved us. Hanna, Jackie, Jellyfish, Aunt Peggy. They loved us, they held us up, they gave us sanctuary in my mind, at least in this moment. "It makes me remember that some people do care."

"That's the idea," said Dad. "They number more than those who don't."

"It's hard to remember that."

"That's the point of the cookie." He held out the keys to the van. "Want to drive?"

I backed away. "I've never driven a van."

"It's not any harder than any other car. Just take your time. Ease into it. There's not much traffic on this road." Then, "Shoot." He withdrew the keys. "I forgot. You don't have your permit." He heaved out a breath. "You better not drive if you don't at least have that." He heaved out another breath.

"Wait." I opened the passenger side door and bent to pull my wallet from underneath the seat. I took out the permit and waved it at him.

"You didn't leave it at home? You've had it the whole time?" Dad laughed. A loud, hearty laugh. I didn't think it was that funny. "Where was it when you showed us your empty wallet?"

"In my shoe."

"In your shoe?"

"I wasn't going to give it to Mr. Oberman. It's mine. Mom was with me when I got it."

Dad laughed hard again, even harder.

"Why are you laughing like that?"

"Oh, I don't know. All that security, and you hide your permit in your shoe. Same as the bank card I just used. The FBI and the marshals—apparently they don't know about that account, and I'm fine with that."

"The card was in your *shoe*?" I felt incredulous. "In your *shoe*? Dad!"

"Look who's talking."

"But, Dad!"

He just shook his head and laughed some more. "I don't know what we are," he said, "but we are certainly some pair."

"But why did you hide your bank card? The FBI wasn't going to keep your money."

"Maybe I was afraid things wouldn't work out so great if we depended completely on them. And they haven't, so I guess I'm glad. Well, you want to drive?"

"My permit's in the wrong name, and it's probably been canceled."

"I don't care," he said. "Use the permit. It is yours."

"But what if we get stopped?"

"What if we do?"

I still felt unsure. "I suppose nobody will actually look at it if I don't speed or hit anything."

"And you won't," said Dad. "You'll be careful. But it gives us a little insurance if you have a permit. We can relax a little more if you have something you can show. If showing it tells the FBI where we are, we'll deal with it then."

So I drove. The first time since Mom had died.

At first I took short turns at the wheel, driving only on back roads where there wasn't much traffic, and when there was, I pulled over and waited. But before long I wasn't pulling over.

How many days did we drive? I lost count. It just felt like:

Drive.

Motel.

Drive.

Motel.

A few days into it I started getting those flashbacks whenever we stopped, even though I was right there with Dad.

Bang-fall! Bang-fall! It was like a fever that rose when the hum of the car stopped. Just not knowing where we were going or if we'd be safe there—that was the only reason I could think of. I guessed I'd felt safe in Kansas. I hadn't been. We hadn't been.

"Put your seat back, Liza," Dad said to me the first time I got the flashback after driving. We weren't even out of the van yet. "Take a deep breath, let the feeling ride over you, and the fear will go away."

He stayed in his seat next to me, looking at maps while my brain ballooned up to the stars and back. He couldn't pat me on the shoulder or hug me or anything while it was going on. For some reason that just made it worse. But the crinkling of the map under his fingers during the episode kept the noise of it down. And Dad was right. The flashback rode over me like a giant wave, peaked, and fell away.

Drive.

Motel.

Drive.

Eventually the flashbacks eased off and stopped. Sometimes I felt a glimmer of one, like those low notes you hear in a movie when you know something bad is about to happen, but the thing never got organized enough to take over the way it had.

Drive.

Motel.

Drive.

Chapter 15

In one of the motels I dyed my hair. Dad had bought the package in a pharmacy, and I studied the coloring directions from one of the beds while he opened his computer.

"Good thing you had that with us when we took off," I said.

"Yeah," he answered. "Lucky twice with this. First when Detective Sawyer suggested I bring mine from the house, and then having this new one in the car when we went to the library. I think I'll keep it tied to my wrist from now on."

Dad settled down to work, and that made me smile. He looked up and caught the smile.

"What?"

"It just feels good to see you working," I said. "It feels good to have something normal happening."

He nodded. "Soon it will be most things," he said. "Soon. Nothing stays this intense."

While he worked, I camped in the bathroom with the hair dye.

It stunk! But afterwards I was black-haired. I stared at the mirror, trying to make my new look compute. That was me?

I dried my hair and combed it before coming back out to where Dad was still working. "What do you think?"

He looked up from the screen.

"You look good," he said. "I'll have to get used to you with dark hair, but it's good. Almost matches your eyebrows."

"We can buy a black eyebrow pencil for them," I said. "My eyebrows won't be *almost* black then. They'll *be* black. No more red, period."

So I wasn't red-haired anymore, and with that change and the one to my eyebrows, we both felt a little more comfortable.

"I think," said Dad before we set off the next morning, "we can stop running. We can find a place to live."

"Agreed. But what about our names?"

"We'll stay with Harvey and Linda Weston. We have those IDs."

Nobody would pick me out from the crowd now. I was still tall, but that was the only thing that made me much different, at least visibly, from everybody else. I'd stay away from basketball courts for a while. No one needed to see me shoot a three-pointer anytime soon. But would it matter? Who would care?

Somewhere in Ohio we found a town we liked. Just the way it looked with the neatly painted front porches and pine trees. Comfortable. Quiet. What else could we go on?

We bought some sandwiches and drinks at a mini-mart and took them to a park with a creek running through it, picnic tables placed nearby. Some geese.

"This is nice," I said. "Peaceful." It was the most relaxed I'd felt in a long time. How long? It hadn't been that many weeks since Mom's death, had it?

"We could use some peace." Dad popped open his soda and took a long drink. "Ahh!"

We ate our sandwiches and watched the geese. They found us boring and didn't even honk at us. Fine with me. I kind of liked being boring, even if it was only geese I bored.

Honk, honk, honk! A flurry of wings. We watched the geese rise and disappear over the trees. *Honk, honk, honk, honk!* Their honking faded, and I looked at Dad.

"Was it something we said?" I asked.

"We'll choose our words more carefully next time," he answered. "We don't want to insult the geese."

The world returned to silence while we ate. Then *snap!* *Snap-snap!* Twigs breaking.

I stood up. Which way, which way?

Snap! Snap!

Dad and I sprinted to the van.

Snap!

Could we get out fast enough?

I had the door open and was half inside the van before we saw them.

Joggers.

My whole body sagged with relief.

That's all it was.

Joggers, a whole crowd of them, running through, following a path we hadn't even noticed along the creek.

"Hi," a man breathed at us as he went by.

Dad nodded, and I said hi back. Another jogger, a lady, smiled, and her face made me think she was working so hard to run that it was hard for her to do even that. We watched as the joggers disappeared into the woods.

Just joggers.

Harmless.

I wished the joggers hadn't come by. But I guessed it was all right. We were still safe, and they were just joggers doing what joggers do. Acting like regular people. I tried to get that relaxed feeling back. I couldn't let myself be afraid of *everybody*.

"The geese liked us all right," commented Dad. We sat down again. "Just not them."

"What's not to like?"

Dad put his trash into the bag our lunch had come in and took one last swig of his soda.

"I like this place," he said. He took in a deep breath and let out a good sigh. *Ahhh-huhhhh!* "I guess I should call Mr. Swensen," he said. "He's probably wondering what happened to us."

Susan Shaw

"I thought we weren't letting him know anything. I thought we were doing this on our own."

"We can't," he said. "I'm thinking a little more clearly than when I smashed the phone. We need his help. We can't stay in hotel rooms every night. I've had to go to the bank twice now, you know. The money won't last forever. Besides, you're supposed to testify. How can you do that if the FBI and the marshals don't even know where we are? How can they protect us?"

"We can blend in here, and nobody even has to know," I said. "And I don't care about testifying anymore. I just want to hide."

"I wish it was that simple," said Dad, "but—"

"Oh, man," I said, and my heart sank, "there's always a 'but.' There's always got to be a 'but'!"

"I know, and I'm sorry, but Gary Carmichael found us in Kansas. Who knows how? He could find us here. We need the protection. And we need help to find a place to stay."

I felt unhappy. "Where was the FBI in Kansas?" I asked. "Or the marshals? We were lucky to get out of there. If we'd been five minutes sooner . . ." I bit my lip, knowing too well what that would have meant. "That was lucky."

Dad nodded. "I'm not going to argue with a little luck," he said.

"But the FBI and the marshals service," I said, "why didn't they know?"

"They can't know everything."

"I guess not. Anyway," I said, "it was the pictures."

"The pictures?"

"In the newspaper and the magazine and on TV. That's what led Gary Carmichael to us. I don't know how, exactly, but it had to be that, and the FBI couldn't do much about the pictures. Although they could have warned us once those pictures were out."

Dad nodded. "Perhaps they figured we were safe on a Kansas farm anyway. Who'd look for us there?"

"One of the farm customers probably ID'd us." I wondered which one. Tonette? She'd driven her car in front of Carmichael's. Maybe she'd been leading him to us.

But I didn't believe that. She was just going home or to the farm for more milk.

How likely was it, anyway, that Tonette or Ponytail-man or anyone in the middle of Kansas actually knew Gary Carmichael? But if not one of them, who?

"Now I don't match the pictures," I went on, "and you never did. They were terrible pictures of you. They made you look like a dinosaur or something."

"Ah, so sad, so sad. My one chance to get a big modeling contract, and I looked like a dinosaur." Dad struck a he-man pose, his biceps flexed. "I'll retire from teaching and just model." He reversed the pose, looking the other way. "What do you think? Should I call a photographer for a second chance?"

I burst out laughing and did a glamour-girl pose back at him, one hand on my head and one on my hip.

"I'm disappointed too," I said. "Now I'll never break into modeling."

"Well, clearly," said Dad, "the world has missed its chance with us. It may never come again."

I went back to my sandwich. "You know," I said between mouthfuls, "I didn't see in any of the articles about your two different-colored eyes. But what if it was there?"

He nodded. "You can't really notice that unless you look."

"But if they make that known and somebody picks up on that—"

"We'll worry about that when it happens."

"I just wish I'd dyed my hair in Kansas." I paused. "I kind of liked it in Kansas with Hanna and all. We were already friends."

"I know."

I took one last bite of my sandwich. "Maybe I *would* have liked riding a horse."

"Yeah. Well, maybe somewhere else."

I'd hated the way that felt, having to leave so fast, not even getting to say good-bye.

"Someday," said Dad, and he grinned at me, "we'll look back on all this and laugh."

"When?"

"I don't know." He gazed at the water. "But we will." He flipped open the phone. "I'm going to call Mr. Swensen. See what he has to say."

"You don't have his number, do you? It was in the other phone."

"I can get it."

I left the table. I walked far enough away so that the gurgling of the creek covered what Dad said. I sure hoped Mr. Swensen wouldn't tell us we had to come back to Kansas. I wished he wouldn't say anything, and just leave us alone to start over.

But how could we start over if Dad couldn't teach? What could he do instead? What could I do? I pictured us living in a subway station with a bunch of other homeless people if the FBI money ran out. No. That wasn't going to happen. Dad had his savings, and maybe his latest show would make money. And the FBI money couldn't run out too soon if they knew where we were. Right?

After a few minutes I saw Dad close up the phone, so I came back. "Well?"

"He was mad," said Dad. "Really mad. I learned some new words that mean 'idiot.'" He shrugged. "I don't blame him."

"So he won't help us?"

"Oh, he will. First, though, he had to swear at me."

"He swore at you?" Nobody ever swore at Dad.

"I'll live." And then he told me, "We only have to spend one more night in a hotel. Then there's a house right here."

"Right here? *Here?*"

"Well, ten miles away. But the U.S. Marshals Service is all over. Mr. Swensen thinks we can get in tomorrow."

"They don't have to check or anything?"

"I guess he looked in some database."

"They haven't used this place before, have they?"

"I don't think so. The owner died a few months ago, and the son wants to rent it."

"Sounds like luck," I said.

"It's nice to finally have some luck."

Hm. Luck. I was okay with some of that.

Chapter 16

U.S. Deputy Marshal Dexter Treves came from Cleveland the next day and took us through the house.

The house didn't have much in it. A couch, a couple of beds, and a card table with some folding chairs in the dining room.

"There's no TV," I pointed out to Dad.

"Houses don't come with TVs," he said. "Even furnished ones."

True, there hadn't been one on the Jones's farm.

"There's a radio." Mr. Treves indicated one that was attached to the bottom of a kitchen cabinet. "That's something to start with." He pointed out the garage door opener mounted just inside the door that led directly from the kitchen into the garage. "And here's the one you can keep in your car," he said, pointing to a boxy plastic object that sat on a counter.

"That will come in handy on a rainy day," said Dad.

"Oh, and I've got you some new IDs and a phone. I'm speed dial one." *Just like Mr. Swensen*, I thought. Probably standard operating procedure.

Now we were the Parkers: Richard and Jennifer from Hoboken, New Jersey, a small town across the Hudson from Manhattan, a town where baseball and Frank Sinatra were both born. I found that out on the Internet later. I'd never been there, and I would never have heard of Frank Sinatra if Mom and Dad hadn't listened to his music sometimes.

"I'm Jennifer? After Liza and Lydia and Linda? How about Louise or Lois or Lillian?"

"We could change your name again if you really don't want to be called Jennifer," said Mr. Treves. "I didn't think the *L* names were giving you much luck. And there are lots of Jennifers out there to blend in with."

"But I don't look like a Jennifer."

"You do now," said Dad. He handed me one of the cards that Mr. Treves had given him. My Ohio learner's permit. Same picture as the one on my Pennsylvania permit, but the hair was dark and described as black, same as on the Arizona one. My hair was finally matching the ID!

"Thanks," I said. "I'm glad to have it." I stuck the permit into my pocket.

Dad put his new license into his wallet and gave Mr. Treves the Kansas one. I noticed he kept the prepaid phone, but that had to be all right. No one could know we even had that except

Mr. Swensen. He was the only one we'd called, and that was only once.

"And about school," said Mr. Treves. "I've sent Jennifer's records—" He glanced at me. Jennifer's records—my records. "I've sent them to the local high school. You can register her for classes anytime. They have all your old grades and all your old teacher comments, Jennifer, just now all coming from Hoboken. Plus we got final grades for you on your last report card. No problem that you didn't quite finish the term."

Funny tremors snaked through my stomach. "It's safe for me to go to school?"

"I don't see why not," said Mr. Treves. "No one knows you're here." He glanced at me again. "I'm glad you finally dyed your hair. It completely changes you from your old pictures."

I touched my hair. It still felt red to me. "I didn't want to."

"I know. Mr. Swensen told me. Just keep dyeing your hair, and everything should be fine."

"School, huh?" Dad looked at me. "We hadn't really talked about that yet."

"Well, you can register anytime."

There was a silence while we took in all Mr. Treves had said.

Dad broke the silence. "Any suggestions?" he asked the marshal. "Other than lying low?"

"That's the best plan I can think of," said Mr. Treves, "other than being observant and staying in touch." His last words were emphatic.

Dad nodded. "We won't disappear again."

"Good. Also, Mr. Parker, you really should do something about those eyes. Do you wear glasses?"

Dad and I looked at each other. So his different-colored eyes did matter.

"Just to read," Dad answered. "I didn't think people knew about my eyes."

Mr. Treves pulled a pair of blue-tinted glasses from his breast pocket. "They're just window glass," he said, "no prescription, but you might want to get tinted contacts. And I wouldn't doubt that the Core knows a whole lot more about you than your eyes. If we know it, they know it. Just assume that."

"Like what?"

"You have perfect pitch."

Dad lifted the corner of his upper lip. "So? Who would care about that?"

"Not me," said Mr. Treves. "But it's a detail. If we know it, they know it. So just think about that when you order your second cup of coffee." The marshal turned his eye to me. "And you like hot chocolate without whipped cream."

I shivered. "Dad!" How did Mr. Treves know that?

Dad glanced at me. "I'm sorry," he said, "but I'm not going to worry about those details. Coffee and hot chocolate with or without whipped cream at our own kitchen table is not very distinguishing. Which is where we'll drink it." He put on the glasses, and his different eye colors were hardly noticeable behind the blue. "Thanks for the glasses."

"That's why we're here," said Mr. Treves. "You might want to grow your hair too."

I thought of Pony-tail man. "Why not?" I said to Dad. "Wear braids."

Dad grinned at me. "I thought I'd go for a dreadlock persona. Start writing rap."

"You don't want to get too extreme and go the other way," said Mr. Treves. "That'll call attention too." Didn't he know Dad was kidding?

Dad winked at me. "Okay," he said. "No dreadlocks." Then he asked, "What about the stuff we left behind in Kansas? It's not much, but I think we'd like to have it. Mostly clothes."

"Don't forget the teddy bear," I added. "And I'd hate to lose the iPod. I told Jeff I'd give it back the next time I saw him." Whenever that was going to be.

"Everything's in a box," Mr. Treves told us. "I'll let you know when it comes in, and you can pick it up from my office."

"Why is it going to you?" I asked.

"This house wasn't cleared yet when they sent it. You'll get it a little faster than if I mailed it to you, but you'll have to drive to get it."

Then he left, and Dad and I did what we could to get settled. Went food shopping, bought sheets and blankets for the beds, some towels, and hats for the two of us that didn't have the Phillies logo on them. Mine was a big and floppy blue one. I liked the idea that I could pull it over my eyes. Dad's hat was a generic baseball cap, also blue, but with a black visor.

Susan Shaw

"I'll give you a ponytail holder when your hair gets long," I said.

"I may take you up on that," he said.

Then we came back to the house and put our new purchases away before unpacking what we'd brought with us into Ohio. It wasn't much. Mostly underwear and socks, some shirts and an extra pair of pants each, so we could do laundry and still have something to wear while we did it. All of it we'd picked up at some anonymous mall about two days into our panicked road trip.

When we were finished, I brought up the lack of clothing to Dad.

"It's dumb to buy what we already own," he said. "We'll just make do until the movers get here."

"When do you think that will be?"

He laughed.

"What?"

"I was thinking," he said, "what it must be like to be driving that truck. The movers thought they were taking our stuff to Kansas. Then we disappeared. Now we're here. Who knows where we'll be when they catch up with us. Hawaii? Alaska? Key West? They're having a tour of the country."

"I hope we're here long enough for them to catch up with us," I said. "I don't want to go anywhere else for a while. Unless it's home."

"You and me both, kid."

It was dinnertime at that point, but neither of us felt like making a big deal of it. Just a couple of sandwiches and hot chocolate.

Maybe things would work out here in Ohio, but, as I kept reminding myself, all this was temporary. Everything we were doing was temporary. We were going home as soon as the FBI caught Gary Carmichael and put him and his pals in jail. How long would that take?

We took our meal into the living room and ate it while we sat on the couch. Dad nodded, looking around the room.

"Not too bad," he said. "Not bad at all."

"It'll work." I rested my head against the back of the couch. "Could be a little homier, but it'll work."

"When the piano arrives, it will feel like home for sure."

"The piano is what it will take?" I asked. Well, lacking Mom. That was understood, but I didn't want to say it out loud. No place could feel like home, not the way it had, since we couldn't have her.

"Play one, and it warms up the wallpaper," Dad said. "Everybody feels better when there's a piano in the house."

I couldn't argue with that.

We finished our meal and went outside to explore the backyard. A patio with a table and two chairs; some gardens near the house; a low hedge between our yard and the neighbors; a few trees, with a birdhouse strung from one; and a fairly good-size grassy lawn.

"I guess we'll have to buy a lawn mower." Dad looked at me. "Sorry." He never could cut the grass because of his shoulder, so Mom and I had always switched off on that chore.

I shrugged. "I don't really mind it. But it looks like somebody's just been here with a mower."

"I'm glad," said Dad. "I won't mind not buying a mower right away, but the next time we go out, maybe we'll get some birdseed. That feeder's empty."

"Don't." That wasn't me.

We turned to see a girl standing in the driveway on the other side of the hedge. She was tall, maybe five-nine, and probably a little older than I was. She held a basketball under one arm.

"Don't," she said again. "Not unless you like the idea of cats catching cardinals in your yard. The people behind you will provide the cats." She paused. "Welcome to the neighborhood. I'm Cassie Magruder."

"Thanks for the tip and the welcome, Cassie," said Dad. "So—no birdseed, no bird hunters."

I stared at the girl. A house when and where we wanted one, and a basketball-playing girl right next to it? How? But the FBI—the marshals—they wouldn't be setting us up? Would they? The girl—she'd be too obvious.

Who didn't shoot baskets at least sometimes, though? Also, I just couldn't believe that this girl, who probably really did live in the next house, could be part of some plot to trap us. She couldn't have moved there on the off chance that we might show up. Mostly I couldn't believe it, but that paranoid part of me sure could. *Stop!*

Dad elbowed me, and we walked closer.

"Hi," I said. We introduced ourselves. Richard and Jennifer Parker. *Jennifer, Jennifer, Jennifer.* Me. Jennifer. Anyone looking at me could see I wasn't a Jennifer. Jennifers were pretty and had long blond hair and blue eyes. They had poise. I was the anti-Jennifer. Brown-eyed, awkward, and gangling, except on the basketball court, and odd-looking. Certainly odd-looking.

Cassie didn't seem to notice that I was the anti-Jennifer.

"Want to shoot some baskets?" She held out the ball.

I looked at Dad. He shrugged at me. "Up to you," he said.

"I'm not very good at basketball," I told Cassie, "but I'll try." Dad turned away at that so Cassie wouldn't notice his stifled laugh. I knew what he was thinking. *She's not very good. Right. Uh-huh. Only better than everybody else.*

Well, he was my dad.

So I went over to Cassie's while he went back inside. I didn't like it, Dad not being where I could see him, but I knew he was right inside, just on the other side of that stucco wall, probably looking straight out at me through the kitchen window while Cassie and I chased each other all over her driveway.

But even if he wasn't, why should I worry? As far as the rest of the world was concerned—except maybe the movers, and what would they care?—we'd disappeared off the face of the earth. We were safe. Who knew where we were really except for Mr. Treves? And he wouldn't tell. Would he? Of course not. And the movers—they probably didn't know who we really were. Did they? Could they be part of the Core?

Stop being paranoid!

It was hard work being bad at basketball, but I made it into kind of a game, always aiming to the right of the sweet spot, tripping over my feet now and then, and always thinking I'd make sure to stay away from the game after this so I wouldn't have to keep pretending. Just for now, though, okay. Just for now.

Between plays Cassie and I talked. It was just her and her mom living in the house, she told me, but her mom was away for the summer taking care of *her* mother while Cassie, two years ahead of me, lifeguarded most days at the local swim club.

"In the middle of August," she added, "I start college. Most of my friends have already started in summer sessions or gone into the military, and it's gotten sort of lonely around here. I'm really glad you showed up."

"And I'm glad you live here and we can be friends right away," I said. "Where are you going to go to college?"

"Ramsey. It's right nearby. I might go into nursing," she told me, "but I'm not sure."

"I can't even think about it," I said. "College, I mean. It seems so far away."

"It comes up fast," said Cassie.

And I told her a little about us, that it was just Dad and me since my mom had died—of pneumonia in the spring. And when Cassie went off to college, I'd be homeschooling with Dad. Dad and I hadn't talked about that, but it was what I wanted.

"I'm sorry about your mom," Cassie said.

"Thanks." I made a shot for the basket, but I missed, not on purpose. Cassie took the rebound, and I went on. "We may not be here long enough to get settled," I said. "Just until Dad finishes his book. Then he might start at another college."

"Another college?"

Oops.

"I mean he might teach somewhere. He's just not sure where yet."

She raised her eyebrows at me. "Is he a novelist?"

I laughed. "No, not that kind of book. He writes—" And I hesitated before my next lie. "He writes art textbooks for colleges." Keep music out of it. Keep Stravinsky and Bach out of it. No Broadway shows, either.

"Oh, does he paint?"

"No." I laughed again. Dad paint? He could hardly draw stick figures. "He's color-blind. But he can write about people like van Gogh."

It was getting dark then, and the mosquitoes were beginning to find us, so Cassie and I quit playing. "Want to come in for a minute?" she asked. "Get something to drink?"

"No, thanks," I said. "I'm sort of shot from the move."

"Okay, next time," she said.

She went inside her house then, and I went across to mine. My house. Our house. Our home. Home. How could this place be our home?

Inside I found Dad, a soda in his hand, lying on the sofa, one leg bent to allow his bare foot a spot on the cushion, and the other stretched out its full length on the carpet while he listened to jazz playing on the radio two rooms away.

I dropped onto the spot next to his hip. "It's kind of tough on us tall people when it comes to lying down on couches, isn't it?" I gestured at his overflowing limbs.

"We manage," he said.

I told him about Cassie and her college plans. "I said I'd be homeschooling with you while you worked on your art text-book." I paused. "I guess we're always going to lie." I shrugged a shoulder. "I probably could have told her the truth. She's probably never heard of Stravinsky. I lied about Mom, too. I said she died of pneumonia in the spring."

"Just as well."

"Also, you're color-blind."

"I'm color-blind? What made you say that?"

"I don't know, one lie leading to another, I guess. I didn't tell her about your two different-colored eyes, at least."

"She's probably figured that one out for herself." He stretched. "So I'm color-blind. Oh, it doesn't matter. Just allow me the ability to walk, okay?"

I laughed. "I was trying to explain why you didn't paint."

"Maybe my book is about color-blind artists. Maybe there is a call for something like that."

I laughed. "Like a book on tone-deaf composers?"

"Yeah. Probably not happening. Well, we won't worry

about it. If Cassie asks, I'll tell her you were misinformed. You're confusing color-blindness with my tone-deafness. That's what I'll say."

I nodded, laughing again. "That would be a logical construct, if incorrect."

"Who's that talking?" asked Dad. "'Logical construct'? 'Logical construct'?"

"I know. It's the Jennifer in me."

"Who?"

"I'm Jennifer now, remember? Blond, blue-eyed, petite Jennifer who knows all the answers."

"That's you all over," said Dad, "especially the know-it-all part."

"Well, get used to it. Jennifer is here."

"Under all that blond blue-eyed stuff, you're still you," said Dad. "Too bad about the name, though. I've always liked the one we gave you. Eliza Jane. *Oh, Eliza, little Liza Jane.*"

I sat there while he sang the tune, and for a minute it felt like Mom was right there, singing along with him. *Oh, Eliza, little Liza Jane. Oh, Eliza, little Liza Jane.* The tune faded into a rising jazz riff from the radio. Then it was just the jazz, and being there. Being there.

At least Cassie was friendly. She was someone I could hang out with, maybe, if she had time. That would help. But we couldn't play basketball together. That was for sure. It was too hard for me to be bad at it, too hard to be that clumsy. Plus I didn't *want* to be that clumsy. I *wanted* to make those shots.

Dribble, dribble, dribble, dribble, dribble, dribble, SHOT! What that could feel like!

What I minded most, though, was the lying. Would it be forever?

Dad's voice broke into my thoughts. "You could go to school," he said. "You could get away with it with that black hair. You don't look so much like the redhead everybody's looking for anymore."

"No." I thought of the flashbacks. What if they returned? I'd still need to be able to find Dad fast and know that the noise inside my head was just noise. I told him that. "Besides," I added, "if we have to run, it's better if one of us can just grab the other and shout 'Go!'"

"We won't have to run again. People are already forgetting about those articles. People always forget. And you're not red-haired anymore."

"Well, there's the rest of the summer to decide," I said. "I could change my mind." I didn't think I would, but who knew?

Then I was suddenly so tired, so tired, so tired, that all of my muscles felt like melting butter. All that driving and feeling keyed-up and scared had drained my energy like a hole in an air mattress, leaving just about nothing behind. Whatever had remained, I'd spent playing basketball with Cassie. Now, sitting next to Dad when nothing had to be done, I could relax a little—oh! No such thing as a little.

I tipped off the couch and stretched out on the floor. I

wished I'd thought to get a book first—what book? Did we have any books in the house? But getting up again to find one felt like more work than I could face. So I just lay there, the music of Charlie Parker and some other jazz gods lulling me as I fell in and out of sleep. It felt good.

Chapter 17

Coffee.

I opened my eyes to the smell of it.

Stripes and squares of brightness—*wait!*—*The sun?*

One of those squares surrounded Dad, who grinned at me over his mug from his place on the sofa. *Cute,* said his eyes.

"Don't say it." I sat up and stretched. "It's morning?"

"Oh, but you are. And it is morning."

"How'd it get to be morning?"

"I think that the sun did its usual trick and sneaked up from the east."

I stretched. "I slept so well! You know, I feel like I can finally relax."

"If you slept well on that floor, that's a good sign."

I cleaned up for the day—showered, found some less than

completely dirty clothes, and put them on. Had breakfast. Toast from last night's loaf of bread.

Afterward Dad and I drove out to the supermarket for a few things we'd forgotten the day before. Cereal, juice, milk, more bread, and cheese. Apples, some frozen vegetables. On the way out of the supermarket, we grabbed the last copy of the *Plain Dealer* from an honor box, and I opened it as Dad started the van.

"Oh."

Dad put the van in park and looked across at me. "What is it?" But he knew. I could just tell.

I showed Dad the picture—my hair screaming its way across the page. And the headline: WHERE ARE THEY NOW?

"That just about nails us," I said.

Dad took the paper from me and looked at it, shaking and shaking his head. "All right, then," he said. "We're homeschooling you for sure." He handed back the paper and took us out onto the road. "I should have figured on this." He shook his head again. "I was stupid to think any place would be safe with that reward out on us. I was living in a fairy-tale world."

"At least nobody knows we're here," I said.

"Yet." He kept shaking his head. "I'm sorry. I'm really sorry, Liza."

"Why are you sorry? I mean, I'm sorry too, but you sound like you're apologizing."

"I am. For talking like everything would be okay because we're here, like nobody would look for us in Ohio. Like you can

Susan Shaw

go to school like everybody else, and life can be normal." He stopped talking, but the head-shaking continued.

"But why should anybody look here? There's the whole world out there. Why find us here?"

"Why'd anyone find us in Kansas? But with that reward, people will look. People will pay attention."

"Anyway, you've got your tinted glasses, and I've got black hair."

"Yup. At least there's that." He let out a deep breath and we continued on home in silence. Mad silence.

Funny, I thought. We were mad and unhappy about what was in the paper, but there was no panic this time, what we'd felt at the library in Kansas. Just the feeling of a downer. And acceptance. I shook my head too. What else could either of us do? It was the way it was.

Back at the house we looked through the newspaper more thoroughly, spreading it all over the living room floor. All those pictures of us, our house in Avon, some of the neighbors, including Jellyfish. A few of the photos were from the Wichita library parking lot, one a direct shot of Dad, so clear. The difference in the color of his eyes was obvious.

But what made the back of my neck prickle was the black-and-white shot. My heart beat fast, and my breath came in ragged shallows as I took in the dark red hair that now equaled black. *Huh! Huh!* I couldn't get my air.

"I was all right a minute ago." *Huh!* "What's the matter with me now?" *Huh-huh!*

"Lie down," Dad said. "Let the feeling ride over you like the flashbacks did. It'll leave in a minute."

So I flattened out where I was, on the floor next to the newspaper, and stared at the ceiling. Cobwebs up there. "But why?" I asked. My heart thumped hard against my ribs. And that ceiling. The ceiling was up there, but it pressed and pressed against my chest anyway.

"Sometimes it takes a little time for our emotions to catch up with our brains." He sounded so calm. "Take deep breaths."

"It feels awful."

"You'll remember in a minute that we're okay."

"Are we?"

"Let's just assume we are."

I lay staring at the cobwebs, trying to get my breath, willing my heart rate to slow down. Slow, slo-o-ow. But were we okay? Slo-o-ow.

Finally things seemed to settle. Somewhat.

I turned my head and saw Dad stretched out on the floor too, on the other side of the papers from me, his chest rising and falling with his own deep breaths. Maybe not so calm. He turned his head and looked at me. Grinned. I grinned back and sat up. He did too.

"Better?" he asked.

"I guess. You?"

"I'll live."

"What was that? I felt for a minute like I was jumping out of my skin."

"Now, that's a scary thought. A skinless Liza. Don't let me ever see that."

I laughed. But then I looked at the papers again, and that prickly feeling returned. Was anybody watching? I felt someone, maybe Gary Carmichael, maybe Robert Bramwell, maybe some other shadowy figure from inside the underpass, staring through the window at us, but when I looked, no one was there.

Didn't matter. I got up and closed the curtains anyway.

"I just don't like the feeling of it," I explained to Dad. "What if someone looked in and saw these pictures and us at the same time?"

"Unlikely," he said, "but having the curtains drawn works for me."

We had a silence where, I guess, we were both thinking, just registering the latest addition to the mess we lived in. How could these things keep happening?

"I don't think anybody could look in that open window without us hearing him climb up onto the porch," added Dad. "And what if someone did? What then? What could that prove about us? We're two people looking at a newspaper."

"Yeah, but it's the idea." I pointed to the paper. "And look, Dad, look at that picture." The one of him from the library. "It's so obviously you. Nothing generic about it." He glanced at the photograph while I went on. "And here." I put my finger on the black-and-white one of me. "It could be me today. What can I do?"

"Nothing," he said. "People will look at that black-and-white picture and mentally paint the hair red because of all the other pictures. They won't connect it with what you look like today."

"Are you sure?"

"No. But it's my best thought. We're just going to have to be careful."

I turned to where the story continued, and Robert Bramwell's picture looked back at me. Apparently word had leaked out that I'd identified him as Mom's killer. Where were we? And why was Robert Bramwell walking around loose? That's what everybody wanted to know. Or at least the person who wrote the article seemed to think so.

And I wanted to answer: *Mind your own business!* What kind of trouble was this reporter giving us?

Jellyfish's name caught my eye. Cameron Carter. Who ever called him that? Although I thought it was kind of a nice name. Cameron Carter. I'd written it all over the inside of my English notebook way back in November, making hearts out of the vowels. I'd never called him that to his face, but it'd felt good saying it, looking at it in print. Cameron Carter. Cameron and Liza sitting in a tree. I'd written that inside a blue ink heart. With three smaller inked-in hearts around it.

Jellyfish. Would I never see him again? Jackie'd told me he thought I was bubbly, that I'd made his whole week because I was so bubbly when we'd won that basketball game. He liked me. He really liked me.

Ohhhh, Jellyfish!

Robert Bramwell was quoted in the article. *The police will tell you that I was in Atlantic City at the time of the tragedy. I am not a murderer.*

"Man," I said to Dad. "I can't even make a mistake. Isn't there something we can do so people don't bother him?"

"Bramwell's a big boy," Dad said. "Leave it to the FBI."

I felt bad and thought of writing Bramwell a letter.

"No."

"But, Dad—"

"Just no. A letter could be traced to wherever you mailed it. Same as a phone call. You could send a message through the FBI to Mr. Bramwell, maybe, but I'd rather you didn't. The quieter we are, the better."

"But why would Mr. Bramwell want to trace my letter if he's innocent? Why would he want to hurt me?"

"Maybe we shouldn't assume he's innocent," said Dad.

"Oh, Dad."

"You identified him from the underpass."

"Dad!"

"You did."

"But, Dad, I messed up. When Mom died, I think I could have said anything. It's a wonder I didn't say the person in the underpass was Brad Pitt or Johnny Depp. Or Ms. Mallory, for that matter."

"Who's Ms. Mallory?"

"My high school principal."

"Never did like her."

"*Dad!* I messed up. I'm sorry. I should remember who I saw. I just don't."

"Let's just say I believe you, even if you don't."

"Oh, Dad."

I thought back to the underpass and the man with the reaching, curling fingers and how I was trying *not* to look at him or any of the others. If only I had!

Chapter 18

A couple of days later we got the call from Mr. Treves that our box had been delivered from Kansas.

"Let's go." Dad handed me my sunglasses and hat. He was wearing the glasses from Mr. Treves.

"Movie-star mode?" I asked.

"Movie-star mode," he answered. He hit the garage door opener, and we went through to the garage, where Dad handed me the van keys.

"My turn?" I asked.

"I kind of like being chauffeured around by my daughter. Turns the tables on you just a little bit."

"Ha!"

After a time Dad directed me onto a ramp of the interstate. I'd driven on interstates before, but this one had concrete

Jersey barriers that took away the shoulders and narrowed the lanes.

"I don't like this." I gritted my teeth.

"Take a deep breath," Dad said. "You're doing fine."

I took a bunch of deep breaths, and I did okay, just didn't love it. Fortunately, there wasn't much traffic, but I was sure going to be glad when we got past the barriers. When would they end?

"I wonder why they call them Jersey barriers," I said.

"I don't know," said Dad. "Maybe—"

A purple car shot around us at high speed, then cut in front of the van. I jammed on the brakes so I wouldn't hit it, and screeched toward the passing lane, the only place to go. The driver of the other car shot forward again and disappeared around a curve.

"Man!" I was out of breath.

"What an imbecile! You all right?"

Before I could answer, another car, a blue one, came up behind us, tailgating and honking before also swerving around me. And then there was the purple car again, waiting on a temporary pull-off before it came up honking behind the van. The honking car, I saw in the rearview mirror, had a couple of people in the front seat. They were laughing. Laughing hard.

The car got closer to my bumper, closer and closer. *Honk-honk-honk-honk-honk-BANG!* The van lurched under us. The occupants of the purple car laughed harder on the impact. *Bang!*

Susan Shaw

Again. Again they roared. It was the funniest thing in the world to them.

I tried to pass the blue car to get away, but it moved as I moved and stayed on the line between the lanes. I was trapped.

"He's going to hit us again," said Dad.

Bang!

An exit coming up. Could we last that long? *Bang!* And again. *Bang!* We got to the small opening, and I peeled off as the car behind us—*Bang!*—hit us again. Too fast, too fast. I struggled for control.

Dad's head faced the rear. "They couldn't react fast enough to follow us. Good job!"

Finally I could slow down. Then I pulled over onto the shoulder and stopped. I let out a deep breath, then another. I took my fingers off the steering wheel and put them over my face, through my hair. Another deep breath.

"That was close," said Dad. He closed his eyes.

Deep breath, deep breath. "Was that the Core, do you think?" Deep breath.

"I wouldn't doubt it."

"We could have died."

"I don't think they cared."

"Did you see what they looked like? I remember the laughing, but I can't tell you what they looked like. Just big, open, laughing mouths. And I never saw the guy in the blue car. Not his face."

"They were young guys," said Dad. "Maybe college age. Not Gary Carmichael."

"Here." I handed Dad the keys. "I never want to drive again."

We switched seats and I tilted mine back so that I was looking at the ceiling. "I bet it was the Core," I said, "trying to kill us. Trying to make me lose control of the van and crash into one of the barriers. It wouldn't look like murder."

Dad started the engine. "Well, you outsmarted them. You and your sixteen-year-old reflexes. You did a great job back there."

"You think so?"

"Absolutely. You're the hero of the day." He pulled the van back onto the ramp. "We'll go the rest of the way off the interstate. It can't be very much farther, and I'd rather drive a thousand miles out of the way than get back on that road."

"What isn't very much farther?"

"Mr. Treves's office."

"Oh, yeah. I forgot we were going there."

We traveled the rest of the way on the ramp before Dad stopped the van again to consult a map. Then we went on, and it wasn't long before we arrived at the offices of the U.S. Marshals. Hurray!

We climbed out of the Caravan and went around to look at the bumper. All smashed in. You couldn't even see the original dings. Dad looked at me and shook his head.

"Again," he said, "you are the hero of the day."

We went inside and told Mr. Treves about what had happened on the highway.

"Did you get a license plate number?" he asked.

"Did you, Dad? I didn't even notice a license plate."

Dad frowned. "I did see the one in front of us," he said. "Wait." He paused. "It's a girl's name." Mr. Treves and I watched while Dad stared at the ceiling. "*N-O-R-A*." He paused. Then he gave three numbers. "It was an Ohio plate."

"I'll call that in," said Mr. Treves.

"Do you think it was the Core doing that to us?" I asked.

"It could have been. We'll find out who was driving that car—what, half an hour ago?"

Dad looked at his watch. "That would have been about it."

"Okay. I'll take care of it." Mr. Treves picked up his phone and spoke into it while Dad and I waited. Mr. Treves basically said what we'd told him, then hung up. "I'll let you know as soon as I hear anything," he said. "Do you want to hang around here until I do?"

Dad looked at me. "Liza?"

I shook my head. "I think I just want to be outside somewhere. Moving."

"I don't see what's wrong with that idea," Dad said. "Those people don't know where we went after we got off the highway, and we'll take our time getting home."

"I'll send someone over to your house," Mr. Treves said, "just in case there's some funny business. Don't go back until I call you."

"Fine," said Dad. "We've got some errands to run anyway."

"You don't think it's the Core," I asked, "do you?"

Mr. Treves shook his head. "No, I don't."

"Why not?"

"What happened to you on the highway sounds like a dangerous prank. The Core doesn't play pranks."

"Some prank."

Dad cleared his throat. "How about that box you're holding for us? That is why we came."

Mr. Treves pointed to his desk, where a cardboard box sat. "There you go." It wasn't a very big one.

"That's it?" I asked. "That's it? We practically get killed for that one little box?"

"There couldn't have been much to put into it," said Dad, "but what about the stuff from our house in Pennsylvania? When are we getting that?"

"It should be soon."

"Any word on the sale of our house and cars?"

"The cars have sold, and there's some interest in the house, but no takers so far."

I made a face. No matter what the news was, I wouldn't like it. What I wanted—keeping our house and the cars, Mom's Honda with the rose pin on the sun visor—that wasn't going to happen. We couldn't even keep the pin!

Dad nodded. "Good to know. All right. The box." He made a motion for it.

"I got it, Dad."

The box wasn't very heavy, and Dad could have handled it, but I took over, muttering something about Dad's shoulder as

Susan Shaw

I did. Really, I just wanted to carry it. Do something that made sense. Pick up the box, carry it to the van, put it inside, and have it be there.

Dad suggested we unpack the box in the back of the Caravan to make sure it wasn't somebody else's stuff. "I don't want to have to come back," he explained.

Nope. It was ours, all right, and most of the room was taken up by the teddy bear Ms. Harris had given me. Bathing suits, underwear, a couple of outfits for both of us. Jeff's iPod with its cord tangled up in one of my sneaker laces.

"They forgot the sheets and towels," Dad said. "Oh, well. I guess we can just call them gifts to the Joneses. Brand-new except for one day's use."

"They deserve some kind of thank-you," I said.

"Yeah, but usually a gift doesn't require the giftee to strip beds and run a load of wash. Oh, well. At least the Joneses have a story to tell about the strange tenants who stayed for a day and left a deposit of dirty sheets and towels. And all that food in the refrigerator."

"The story of weirdos from the East," I said. "That was the real present."

I untangled the iPod's cord and put the earphone into an ear.

"So you're complete again?" Dad grinned at me.

I grinned back and turned on the iPod. Nothing. Then I saw that the case was cracked. I showed it to Dad.

"I don't think it was like that when we left."

"Could be a dead battery," he said. "Either way, we can hardly complain about a gift. I noticed a RadioShack on the way here, though. Let's stop there and see if we can get the iPod fixed. If not, we'll get another one sometime."

"I do have one coming from Avon," I reminded him, "supposedly."

"Still," said Dad. "it would be nice if you could have this one now."

I headed for the passenger seat. Would I ever want to drive again? Dad took his place behind the steering wheel and turned on the ignition.

While he drove, I tried the iPod on the car's stereo system. Nope. Wouldn't work there, either.

"Oh, well," I said, and tossed it onto the backseat. "I guess it's trash." I slouched down. Stupid thing!

"Let's not go into full mourning before we try RadioShack."

"I know," I answered. "It's not the end of the world. It's just that I want it to work now. I want *something* to be right."

"Maybe it can be fixed on the spot."

But it couldn't.

"Hm!" The man at the RadioShack looked at it. I hid in the background behind my floppy hat and sunglasses. Dad had taken off his hat, but he still wore the tinted glasses that Mr. Treves had given him. I guessed that's how it would be forever, wherever we went. "Well, maybe we can fix it, but we send everything out."

"That's fine," said Dad. "I'll call you—say, in a week?"

The clerk took down Dad's information, which I was close enough to hear. As far as the clerk was concerned, we lived on Seventh Street in Cleveland. Southwest Seventh Street. And the phone number was total fiction.

Then, without the iPod, we returned to the parking lot.

"*Is* there a Seventh Street in Cleveland?" I had one foot inside the van, the other on the pavement while I faced Dad, just on the other side of my door.

"Bound to be," answered Dad. "Every city has a Seventh Street. Whether there's a *Southwest* Seventh Street in Cleveland, I don't know."

"Liar."

"I *don't* know."

"I mean generally."

"Yeah, well, better that than dead."

"That clerk wasn't going to kill us."

"Good. You may now marry him."

"Ha. Do we have to lie about everything?"

"I never thought I'd say this to my own child," said Dad, "but yes. We do. We have to do whatever it takes to survive. If it takes lying, then we lie. If it takes stealing, then we steal. If it takes killing, then we—"

"Dad!"

Dad stared down at the pavement and shook his head. "I know," he said. "I've become a savage. But I'm not going to let some slug just take my daughter away from me. Not my wife and my daughter, too." He looked up at me again. "Sorry, little one. I'm still upset over what happened on the interstate. About everything."

"But, Dad, we don't want to kill people."

"Or course not, but we won't just let them waltz in and kill us, either, will we?

"No." I shook my head too. "No."

"And we'll fight. If that means someone like Gary Carmichael ends up dead, I'm not going to go around being upset about it."

The van keys shook in Dad's hands, and he handed them to me. "I don't feel like driving," he said. "Do you mind?"

I didn't want to drive either, but he didn't want to more than me, so I switched seats with him. Before I started the ignition, I gave Dad a good look. His head was tilted back, and his eyes were closed behind the glasses.

"You all right in there?" I asked.

"I will be in a minute," he said, and he opened his eyes. "Sometimes it all just kind of gets to me."

I turned on the ignition. "Me too."

Chapter 19

We started in the direction of home, but we knew we couldn't go there yet.

"So, where?" I said to Dad. "You want to get some ice cream? Celebrate our survival?"

"Personally," said Dad, "what I want is coffee and coffee and coffee, so strong you need scissors to cut it."

"Then, let's get that. First we should stop somewhere and buy some scissors. They're not usually part of the menu."

"I keep a spare pair in my wallet," Dad said, "for just this kind of crisis. Coffee without scissors! I can't even contemplate such a thing. What's wrong with these coffeehouses?"

"I can't imagine," I said. "But if you have the coffee scissors, all we need now is a place that sells cuttable coffee. Where's that?"

"Mmmm. Never mind. I'll wait until we're home."

And I knew he was remembering what Mr. Treves had said about how the Core would know about even his coffee drinking. And if people from the Core were around . . . They *had* to be around. They had to be the pranksters! They might spot us, *would* spot us, would *definitely* spot us in a coffee shop. If they were around.

No, maybe they weren't around. Probably weren't.

But they were. Or maybe were. The pranksters—

So okay about the coffee. And the ice cream. And the*hamburgers*and the*frenchfries*and the*everythingelses*.

Calm, calm, I told myself. *Take a deep breath. Stop being paranoid. The pranksters weren't from the Core. Just a bunch of mindless jerks.*

"So," I said to Dad, and my voice was okay, "since I'm driving anyway, where would you like to go?"

"Let's take a detour to the high school," Dad said, "and sign you up for homeschooling. We'll get that out of the way."

"Can't we sign up over the phone?" My voice sounded kind of whiny, even to me. "I mean," I said, trying to use a more upbeat tone, "wouldn't it make just as much sense? Then we wouldn't have to worry about being recognized."

"No one's going to recognize us, anyway," Dad said. "The average person is just not on the lookout for FBI witnesses, even those with their pictures in the newspaper. And you'll keep your hat on with that brim over your eyes."

"But can't we *try* doing it over the phone? Then we won't have to worry about any of that."

"Nope," said Dad. "They like to see proof of residency, things like that. I couldn't sign you up for kindergarten, I remember, without showing my gas bill."

"But why would we lie?"

Dad looked at me over his glasses. "That's an interesting question coming from someone who's learning to lie about everything including the color of the sky."

"I haven't lied about that yet," I said. "Besides, if we're going to lie to the school people anyway, why can't we do it over the phone?"

"Is that what we should say when we explain to them why we don't want to come in and show them our gas bill? That since we're lying anyway, they might as well listen to our lies over the phone?"

"But I don't want to go," I said. "Can't you do it without me? And anyway, I bet you don't have a gas bill with you. Our house doesn't have a gas line."

"I have something Mr. Treves gave me from the electric company," he said, "showing that the account is in our name. I put it in my wallet along with my license and whatever else he gave me when he took us into the house."

"Uhhhh! Oh, Dad, why do you have to be so prepared?"

"It must be the Boy Scout in me."

"But why do I have to go?"

"You're the student. They might want you to take a test or something, maybe to see if your three years of French is the same as theirs. Or see if maybe you need reading help or to talk about the swim team. It's just easier."

"Oh, all right." We went on for a few minutes without talking. Then I started again. "Why do we have to sign up, though? Why can't we just homeschool and not tell anybody? Like I haven't been born? There must be people like that, maybe in remote areas, who never get reported even when they're born and don't have Social Security numbers and don't go to school. And nobody knows it. They just live. What difference does it make?"

"It makes a difference if you want to go to college. You can't just show up on a college campus. You need records to apply."

"But if this is a record, someone might trace us."

He said one word. "Jennifer."

"What? Oh, yeah. Jennifer from Hoboken. All fiction."

"Right. We won't use the record if we're afraid. But you might be glad you have it. By the time you graduate, the whole Core deal could be a thing of the past, and you could be flying on with your life. Maybe even playing basketball again."

I didn't have any more answers for him, or questions, either, that would stop us from registering, so I just continued to drive. Maybe it wouldn't make any difference. Who at the school was going to care who I was? Just register the girl and go on to the next thing.

Anyway, it was summer. Maybe nobody would be at the high school. Maybe they didn't work mornings in July. Maybe—

Well, it didn't matter. I'd just drive us there, and we'd see.

Eventually, following Dad's directions, I pulled the van into the almost empty parking lot of a red brick building, and parked. Before we could step onto the pavement, the phone Mr. Treves had given Dad rang. Dad looked at it.

"Mr. Treves." Who else? Dad flipped the case open. "Hello? . . . Yes. I see. . . . Is that right? Huh! Thanks. Appreciate it." He hung up and looked at me. "What happened on the interstate was a prank. A dare. A bunch of drunk kids."

"How do they know?"

"They were caught pulling the same thing on some other young girl. Everybody's fine, but those drivers are in trouble."

"It wasn't the Core, then?"

"It wasn't the Core."

"So," I said, "it was just random. A coincidence. We're safe."

A strange giddiness began to ooze up through my swampy paths of thinking. *Ha, ha, ha! Sob!* We were safe! *Sob!*

I studied the building as we started for it, trying to focus my attention there and shake that giddiness. *Don't lose it, Liza!*

To focus harder I silently narrated as though for a documentary: *The brick structure houses both the administrative offices and the high school. Note the date on the left side. Note the lack of windows.*

"I'm not sure I'd like going to this school," I told Dad. "What's wrong with seeing if the sun is shining?" *Sob!* "I always like to see if the sun is shining."

"That could be the auditorium we're looking at," Dad answered, "or the gym. Not that it matters, if you're not going to attend the actual school. They could do the whole thing in windows, and it wouldn't matter to you."

Sob, sob, sob! Silent ones like all the other ones.

I looked up at Dad. "They could do the whole thing in *chicken coops* and it wouldn't matter to me," I said. "Or Cream of Wheat. Or magic wands." *Sob!* That one was audible. "How about coffee mugs?" *Giggle!* "I won't even consider it if it doesn't have coffee mugs built into it. With coffee in each one. And cream and sugar." *Giggle, giggle.* "Measured out exactly the same in each mug." *Giggle, giggle, giggle!*

"Whoa." Dad put a hand on my arm, and we stopped. "Are you all right?"

"Oh, sure, fine." I giggled as I spoke. "I'm so glad we were almost killed by a bunch of drunk kids instead of the Core. It makes us so much healthier." I laughed again.

"Maybe we should wait."

"No. I'm fine. Giddy but fine. I promise to behave. I might laugh, but I'll behave. How, I won't say. But I promise I won't talk about mugs and Cream of Wheat windows and things like that." I stopped talking for a moment, cleared my throat hard to make the giggles stop. "Oh, Dad. I'm so glad it wasn't the Core." I was almost crying, and my voice shook.

He gave my shoulders a squeeze. "I am too. Now pull down that brim so it covers the tops of your sunglasses." I pulled. "A little farther."

I pulled on it again. "I could just wear a bag over my head with a sign that says 'Too Ugly for Prime Time.'"

Dad laughed and shook his head. "Now, little one, that *would* be a lie."

We left the parking lot and entered the building. A uniformed security guard with a name tag—OTTO, it said—met us at the door. So they were open for business.

"We're here to sign up for homeschooling," said Dad.

"Come with me," Otto said, and led us down a hall. The place smelled just like all the other schools I'd ever been in.

"It's that people smell," Dad said when I wondered about it out loud.

I glanced at him. Would anybody notice the two different-colored eyes behind those glasses? I could see it, but I knew to look for it. And what if somebody did notice it? Would they care? Would anybody here put the clue of Dad's eyes together with the news articles? He wasn't the only one in the world with two different-colored eyes. I'd seen them on other people.

He wasn't the only one, same as I wasn't the only tall redhead. Former redhead. So what if two people like us were in the news? So what? And I wasn't a redhead today.

But I was glad Dad was wearing those tinted glasses and I was wearing my hat. I tugged at my hat's brim to pull it even lower over my eyes. The less anyone saw of my face, the better. I just wished I could figure out how to be short, too.

"I had my hopes up for a strawberry shortcake smell," I

said. "What kind of school is this, not smelling like strawberry shortcake?"

Otto half-turned to look at me.

"Sorry," I said.

He turned away again, and Dad cracked a crooked grin at me. "Strawberry shortcake? Wouldn't you settle for blueberry crunch or raspberry parfait?"

"Nope," I said. "Gotta be strawberry shortcake or I'm not coming."

He laughed, and Otto looked back at us again.

"We're a little sleep-deprived," I told him. "We're usually quite reasonable people." The word "reasonable" felt funny rolling off my tongue. I said it again. *"Reasonable."* The *n* sort of stuck to the roof of my mouth like peanut butter—reasonnnable—and the second half of the word was slow in coming out. I giggled.

Otto squinted at my lie. "Lack of sleep can mess with you," he said, and then we stopped alongside a wall with interior windows through which appeared desks and phones and computers, plus a long counter separating all of that from an open area. The school office. "Here you are." Otto opened a door and stuck in his head. "Got a couple of customers for you, Ella."

"Maybe we should take Otto home with us," I whispered into Dad's ear. "Put him on the front porch with a shotgun."

"Maybe you're right," he whispered back. He nodded to Otto as he left the office. "But I'd rather he had a bugle if he's going to camp at our house. Play reveille in the morning and taps at night."

That made me laugh even though it also made me picture Otto hitting Gary Carmichael over the head with his bugle.

"Bugle and piano duets," I murmured, making Dad grin and also making myself not think of Gary Carmichael so much. Keep the joke going.

"We'll put on a recital," added Dad. "Cookies and punch afterward."

"And brownies," I added.

"And brow—"

"May I help you?" asked someone in a slightly elevated voice.

Oh, yeah, Ella, a lady with frizzy gray hair and a pair of glasses worn as a necklace across her chest. She was probably wondering if we were actually going to tell her why we'd shown up or if we'd only come in to whisper to each other in her presence. She folded her hands on the counter between us. But she was a high school secretary. She'd probably seen stranger things.

Dad cleared his throat and put on his serious face to explain why we were there. A minute later Ella had shown us into another office down the hall, where we were welcomed by a nervous little man with a white beard named Mr. Barber. At least, he was shorter than we were. Short with a red shirt and a red knit vest over a big belly. He could have been Santa Claus.

He shook our hands. "How are you—uh-huh, uh-huh, uh-huh. Welcome to our town, uh-huh, uh-huh."

"Is red one of the school colors?" I asked.

"No, uh-huh, uh-huh. Green and white, uh-huh."

"Oh, well, you're wearing a lot of red," I said in explanation.

"Oh." He looked down at himself. "Red. Uh-huh, uh-huh. Just happened to wear it today. I find the school chilly—uh-huh, uh-huh—with the air-conditioning. That's why—uh-huh, uh-huh—I'm wearing a vest."

I felt that giddy feeling rise again with all the uh-huhs, so I retreated to a corner chair to work on keeping the giggles away.

I stared out a window—yes, there was a window—and tuned out the conversation as well as I could so I wouldn't have to hear all the uh-huhs. How could anybody stand to be around this guy?

I shivered in the cooled air. I wished I could have stayed in the car, where it was warmer. Maybe, if Dad had let me, that's what I would have done. I'd have been happy to just sit in the car the whole time, or maybe stand next to it and let the sun warm my face, but maybe I was somehow needed here. Maybe I was supposed to sign something.

No. Dad, it turned out, had to sign something, but not me—*uh-huh, uh-huh*. But maybe Mr. Barber had to actually lay eyes on me. Maybe not. It didn't matter if he had to or not. He did. Well, after the first uh-huhs, he didn't actually look at me, but maybe my presence counted somewhere along the way.

I wished I'd stayed in the car, but no, I didn't. If I'd stayed in the car by myself . . . Well, really, nobody but Dad and I knew where we were. Not really. But anybody could show up in a parking lot.

Or a school.

The idea gave my stomach that uneasy feeling. Who knew where Gary Carmichael really was? He had to be somewhere. Maybe he was here. Maybe he'd had something to do with those cars hemming us in on the interstate. How could we really know? And if he was around there, why couldn't he be in the parking lot of this school? It wasn't such a long drive. Maybe Otto recognized us and called him. Maybe he was on his way. Maybe he was already here, waiting for us in the hall. Maybe—

Stop it! Stopitstopitstopit!

Finally Dad and Mr. Barber finished talking and messing with papers, and Dad touched me on the arm. "Okay, Jennifer," he said. "All set."

Jennifer!

"Okay, Papa Parker," I answered, feeling like the whole name thing was a joke, the way the whole day was turning out to be. I was not Jennifer! No way!

I turned to say something to Mr. Barber like *thank you* or *good-bye* or *see you next time*, but his telephone rang, and he answered it. He waved us off with one of those good-bye smiles that don't meant anything, without really looking at us, not even giving us a parting *uh-huh, uh-huh,* and Dad and I left the room for the hallway. The *empty* hallway.

So.

So much for school and red brick buildings.

Chapter 20

The Treves phone rang while I was still in the kitchen eating my congratulations-you're-alive ice cream, and I heard Dad talking to someone in the living room. Mr. Treves again? But who else? Who else had the number?

I put down my spoon and came out to the living room. Something was going on, for sure. Dad saw me and put up an index finger, so I waited.

"Okay, thanks," he said. "I appreciate that. . . . Sure. Goodbye." Then he put the phone into his pocket and looked at me. "That was Mr. Oberman," he said.

"Mr. Oberman? Back in Philadelphia? Did they get Carmichael? Do they want us to come back so I can testify?"

"No." Dad bit his lip, and I wondered what was wrong. "Remember that other person you recognized in the picture that Mr. Oberman showed you? You know, when you identified Gary Carmichael out of a group shot?"

"He was Charlie somebody."

"Charles McVoy. Well, he's dead."

"Oh." Why tell us? "Should I be sorry?"

"You can be sorry if you want. But he's not just dead. He was murdered. They found him in the Jersey Pine Barrens. And they think he was murdered around the time Mom was killed. He's been missing since then."

I remembered the underpass scene. Everybody laughing and making noise, and Mickey Mouse Man jumping against one of his buddies. *Haw, haw, haw,* went Bramwell's ghost. *Charlie's had too much to drink. Haw, haw, haw!*

"Dad." It was a whisper. "I think I saw him get killed. I think he was stabbed." I cringed at the memory. Oh!

"I thought as much. That's what Mr. Oberman thought too. That's why we got this call. We'll get back to him a little later and tell him. You're right, by the way. McVoy was stabbed."

Knowing for sure made me cringe again. I felt so sad for this man I didn't know, this man who was probably a criminal. But still . . . a life . . . taken like that . . .

We went slowly back to the kitchen. "But I was just walking through the underpass," I said. "They were all just in there, acting like a bunch of awful people. But I was only just walking through. Like a regular person. I wasn't trying to see anything or spy or anything. I was just walking through so I could go home."

"I know, Liza."

"Why don't *they* know that?"

"It doesn't matter if we understand them. We just have to take care of ourselves."

I let out a big sigh. "It's just—so—" I shook my head. "I don't even know how to—" I stopped. "It's all—" I stopped again.

"Do you remember anything else?" Dad asked. "Anything else that happened in the underpass?"

"A car stalled next to me. It was an open convertible. It just stopped dead. That was right before McVoy was stabbed."

Dad and I stared at each other. "It was a setup," I said. "They planned to kill Charles McVoy right there, right then. They dropped him over the railing into the car, I bet. Nobody else was around. Just me, and they kept me from looking back with all the stuff they were saying and doing so I wouldn't look back." The outstretched fingers, the "Hey, girly-girl."

I sat down in front of my ice cream. I didn't want it anymore. I wished I hadn't eaten what I had. Everything felt so weird. Dad filled the teakettle at the sink before turning a burner on under it.

"I saw a murder," I said. "I didn't know it, but I saw it." I pictured Mickey Mouse Man's eyes, how they'd caught the dim light and looked forward, just forward, after he'd jumped. I cradled my head in my arms. "If I'd only known, maybe I could have done something. Stopped them. Maybe he'd still be alive."

"I think he died right away. And you couldn't have done anything to stop it. If you'd tried, you'd have died right then too, and you'd probably be in the Pine Barrens right along with him. You almost ended up there as it was."

I lifted my head. "Oh, Dad! Oh, Dad!" I felt my breath go strange. "Dad!" I crossed my hands against my collarbone and grasped the material of my T-shirt.

"It's okay, little one. They won't get you. I won't let them." And with that firm line that was his mouth, I believed him.

"But why'd they kill him? And why'd they do it there? They were all having a party, all laughing like the Phillies had won the World Series or something. I mean, McVoy even had that silly hat on his head. And he wasn't the only one with a silly hat. It had to be a party."

"These organizations," said Dad. "They have rules we'll never understand."

"Maybe," I said, "McVoy was going to rat somebody out, so they stopped him. Gave him a final party and then killed him. Like a last meal before the death penalty."

"Maybe."

I closed my eyes while Dad moved around the kitchen, getting mugs out, finding tea bags. I could tell by the scrape of the mugs against the cabinet shelf, by the metallic twist when the lid came off the tea canister, a tea canister left half-filled from before we'd moved in. A tea canister like the one Mom had always stuffed her different varieties into.

Comforting sounds. And if there was tea, there was Mom. I

could feel her as long as my eyes were shut. *Liza. Liza the sweet.* I smiled, almost seeing her.

Hi, Mom.

Hi, Liza.

Water ran in the sink, and I listened while Dad washed and rinsed a few dishes, but I didn't open my eyes. Hearing him move around—that was all I wanted. While I just sat, balanced on that chair, not moving to the right, not moving to the left, with Mom's warmth on my cheek. *Oh, Mom.*

"Liza, you look so peaceful."

I opened my eyes as Dad placed two steaming mugs on the table. Sugar in between. And Mom not there, but there. I felt so much better.

"Dad—" I was going to tell him, but I saw those eyes of two colors mist over. He could feel her there too.

I lifted my mug to touch his. "Same as her cookies," I said. "To Mom."

"To Angela."

We drank the bitter brew.

"Ucchch." I made a face and put my mug down. "I really hate tea."

"That's the spirit." Dad scooped some sugar into my tea and stirred. "Drink it. You need it. The sugar and the tea. We both do."

So we sat there drinking tea, two of us who never drank tea. Then the tea was gone and we just sat there.

"Dad," I said, "they're going to kill me. You know that, right? They're going to kill me. There's nothing I can do about it. They'll track us down and kill me. You'll be lucky if they don't kill you, too."

"They are not going to kill either one of us," said Dad. "We're doing everything we can to make sure. And we will succeed. We are at *least* as smart as they are."

I sighed. It was hopeless. "I don't know if it makes any sense to leave or stay," I said. "They're going to find us. Maybe they did already. Maybe those people on the highway—"

"They weren't part of the Core. They weren't."

"I know. But—"

Dad touched my arm. "This will take a little processing, but why don't we do the processing out on the patio? It's a bright sunshiny day. We'll take the paper out there and read it like ordinary people."

"Ordinary people? Ha, ha, ha! When were we *ever* ordinary people?"

"Oh, I don't know," said Dad. "I remember a time back in 1894 that—"

I shoved him on his good shoulder. "Okay," I said. "That's enough!"

We went outside, our hats, my sunglasses, Dad's tinted ones at the ready, because you never knew, you never knew, and we split the paper between us. As Dad had said, it was a beautiful sunshiny day, and we did look like ordinary people on the patio. We looked like them, but we sure didn't feel like them.

"At least," I said to Dad at one point, "now we know why."

He nodded. "There's value in that."

"Hey!" It was Cassie shouting from her driveway. "Jennifer, you want to go to the mall with me?" She came closer to the hedge. "Help me pick out a couple of tops? I have to work later on, so we can't be too long."

I looked at Dad. "Go ahead," he said. "It'll do you good." He handed me the prepaid cell phone. "You won't need that, but you'll feel better with it." He also gave me some money. "Get something silly," he said. "Just no spiders or rodents or anything like that."

"Chicken coops," I said, grinning. I grabbed my hat and sunglasses off the patio table. "Cream of Wheat. And I'm rich, because I still have that twenty dollars from before."

"So go wild," he said. "Buy all the Cream of Wheat you want."

Chapter 21

The car's windows were open as Cassie drove us to the mall. The breeze against my hat made me think of Kansas. So hot there. Hot here, too, but not like Kansas.

"It's nice to be able to have the windows open," I said.

"Good thing," said Cassie, "because the air conditioner needs to be repaired, and I didn't want to pay for it."

"Why pay for it," I asked, "if the air feels this good?"

"Well, there are some days it gets pretty hot. Just not since you've been here. But I can put up with it for the short distances I drive."

I leaned my face into the wind, letting the gentle buffeting take the tension away with it bit by bit. By the time we got to the mall parking lot, I was feeling almost normal.

I couldn't tell Cassie about how I now knew I'd witnessed

Charles McVoy's murder. I wished I could. I could have told her, though, what had happened on the highway earlier in the day, but I decided not to do that, either, because what I most wanted right then was to forget about all of that for a couple of hours. I just wanted to be one of two regular girls doing what regular girls do.

Nothing deadly, nothing scary, nothing serious. Just shop together at the mall and have fun.

Cassie and I went into a couple of stores, and Cassie found some pretty tops, but I didn't see any I liked. I had such a long back, and I wasn't really into the midriff thing. Not every day, anyway. But I saw a pair of really cool earrings at a kiosk.

"Look, Cassie." I showed them to her.

"Oh, wow! What a find!" And Cassie picked out an identical pair. "Karner Blues!"

"What?"

"They're Karner Blues. That's a kind of butterfly."

"You know what they're called? They just look like blue butterflies to me."

"I'm the butterfly girl," she said. "I'll show you my collection some—"

"Hey, Cass!"

We turned around, and approaching was—*Maxwell?* Maxwell from Sea Isle City? What was he doing here? My radar went up, and I searched the faces around me. Had Gary Carmichael and Maxwell been together in Sea Isle City? Was Gary Carmichael here too?

"This is Seth," said Cassie. Not Maxwell? "Seth, Jennifer. Jennifer's the girl I was telling you about who moved in next door." She turned to me. "Seth's my once-in-a-while boyfriend."

"So which is it now?" asked Seth. "Once, or a while?" But not Maxwell? That dimple appeared and disappeared as he spoke just as it had in Sea Isle City. Had to be Maxwell. Maybe Maxwell was his last name. Seth Maxwell. But someone I saw in Sea Isle City was here now? Just a coincidence?

"Oh, I don't know." Cassie's tone was breezy. "What do you think, Jen? Should I give him another chance?"

Seth looked at me with amusement and something else. "She's mad because I lost the watch she gave me. But I found it. See, Cass? See?" He held up his wrist.

"Okay," said Cassie. "It's only a watch, anyway."

Seth slid his arm around her waist. "Ah, honey, honey, honey."

"Sugar pie," said Cassie back, and they gave each other happy smiles before what looked like a really sweet kiss. I looked the other way and wished I'd stayed in one of the stores while they made up. Should I edge away and look in some of the windows?

"Jennifer," said Seth. Oh! Me! I pulled my gaze back. He and Cassie were standing side by side now. "You look kind of familiar. Have we met?" *Uh-oh!*

"I don't see how," I said. "I just moved here." *And if your name isn't Maxwell,* I added silently, *I don't think so.* But it had to be the same guy. No two people looked like that with that dimple and the freckle right over it. Had the Sea Isle City guy had the freckle? I couldn't remember.

I looked away so my hat partially hid my face from Seth. Black hair. I have *black* hair! I wanted to announce. *I'm not the redhead you saw.* But he hadn't seen my hair that day. It had all been hidden inside that goofy hat by the time I'd run into him. And he wasn't seeing my hair right now, either. Was that good or bad?

My eyes took in the expanse of the mall—Oh! Over there, over there! Was that—was that—was that *Gary Carmichael?* My stomach churned. Maxwell here and Carmichael over there. Was I surrounded? Was Cassie in on it? *Had* we been set up when we were given the house we were living in?

I could see only the back of Carmichael's head, but I knew that's who it was. Seth's voice went on and on, but I didn't really hear it. Should I run? Where? Was I safe as long as I was with Cassie? Or was she with the Core?

I reached for the prepaid phone in my pocket.

"Jennifer?" Cassie called out to another friend. She raised her voice. *"Jennifer?"* She touched my arm and I looked into her large green eyes. Oh, yeah. I'm Jennifer.

Gary Carmichael was still there, and my heart beat *Run, run, run!* Where? Would running make it worse? Point me out? Maybe he wouldn't see me if I didn't run. But Seth was here, and maybe Cassie was in on it with him. Could I get away? Could I run to just anybody for help? Who? I squeezed the phone still in my pocket.

"Sorry," I said. "I thought I recognized someone. What?" Then Gary Carmichael turned around. What should I do— where should I go? He would identify me and nod at Seth, and Seth would—

It wasn't Gary Carmichael at all. Somebody else completely.

Relief! My stomach still churned, false alarm or not, and all I wanted to do was go home. Go where no one could look at me. Where no one resembled Gary Carmichael. Where no one could turn out to *be* Gary Carmichael.

Where was that place?

Wait. The wrong guy turned his disinterested eyes so I could look him full in the face. I recognized him. Not Carmichael, but someone else I'd seen in Sea Isle City.

I'd run into him in the motel and hadn't cared a thing about him. The Cleveland Indians guy, the guy who'd called Seth "Maxwell." He'd worn a hat over that bald head when I'd seen him before. But today, boy, he was almost scary-looking with those mild eyes of his.

"Seth asked you a question."

I turned my eyes back to the puzzled eyes of Seth. "Ever been to the Jersey shore?" he asked. "I think maybe I saw you there." He glanced at Cassie. "During the family reunion at my grandmother's." He turned back to me. "You had a really funny hat with streamers coming out of it. In Sea Isle City—a few weeks ago. You ran into me. And you laughed really hard on that concrete bench."

Being in Sea Isle City didn't mean anything, did it? Being

in Sea Isle City when somebody else was there also didn't mean anything. Did it? Anybody in the world could have been in Sea Isle City any day of the year. So I admitted it.

"Yeah, I was there." I wondered what had happened to the hat. Maybe Foxy had kept it. "I recognize you now."

"It's a small world," commented Cassie.

"Seth!" boomed a deep voice near one of the shops. "Do you work here or not?"

"Gotta go, gotta go," said Seth, and he was gone.

Cassie laughed. "That's his dad over there. He owns the cheese shop." We watched Seth join his dad. An older version of Seth. While I watched, the almost-Gary Carmichael stopped to talk with them. "And that's his uncle. He works there too. When they can get him to show up. Mostly he draws pictures of trees and forgets what time it is. Uncle Thaddeus. He does handyman stuff for my mom once in a while."

"I saw him in Sea Isle City too," I said. "He called Seth 'Maxwell.' That kind of threw me off when you introduced him to me."

"Yeah, well, Maxwell's not actually his name, but Uncle Thaddeus calls him that sometimes. It's sort of a joke about when Seth spilled some coffee when he was little. His uncle called him the Maxwell House kid for a long time after that. Then just Maxwell. Mostly."

"The uncle doesn't look like Seth or Seth's dad," I commented.

"Well, it was Seth's mother's family reunion. Uncle Thaddeus is on that side of the family."

We watched Seth with his father and uncle a little longer before turning away.

"Seth's cute," I said. I thought of Jellyfish and wondered what he was doing. "I mean—I know he's your boyfriend, but—"

"You can say he's cute," interrupted Cassie. "That doesn't hurt my feelings as long as you're as trustworthy as I think you are."

"Of course. Did you think we'd see Seth here?"

"Sure. He's here a lot. Hey, want some ice cream?" She pointed. "There's a good place over there."

More ice cream? Sure, except I couldn't get it out of my mind that the real Gary Carmichael could be nearby. It was a false alarm with Seth's uncle, but who was to say that the *real* Gary Carmichael couldn't be in the mall too? Who was to say that the *real* Gary Carmichael couldn't be on the other side of that column over there, and he'd step out from behind it and see me. And he'd have a knife and-and-and-and—

Stop!

"I'm not really hungry," I told Cassie, "and I think I should get home. Since Mom died, Dad gets a little funny if I'm gone too long." A lie. It was me who got funny. A real riot. That's how funny it all was.

"I can understand why."

So we got back into Cassie's car, and she returned us to our neighborhood, chattering about Karner Blues and other butter-flies the whole way.

"Hey." She interrupted herself as we turned down our street. "A moving van."

And it was, parked right in front of our house.

"Now we'll get our stuff," I said. "Finally."

"You don't have your stuff yet? Where has the moving van been all this time?"

I looked at her and rolled my eyes. "Now, that is a very good question."

Cassie laughed and parked the car.

"I suppose I should head over there and get in the way," I said.

"Okay," she said. "I have to get to the pool soon myself."

I said good-bye and cut across the grass to my house. Piano music wafted through the open windows, and I smiled. Dad at the piano, just like normal.

He played two chords—*Ti! Do!*—when I entered the living room, and grinned at me.

"So," I said. "All's right with the world?"

"It's a whole lot better." He lifted something from a box on the floor beside him and handed it to me. "Your iPod from home."

"Oh, good. I like this one more than the one Jeff gave me." I hooked it onto my waistband. "Maybe I'll send his back to him when it's repaired."

"Sounds like a plan. How was the mall?"

I showed him the earrings.

"Pretty," he said. "No Cream of Wheat?"

"I didn't see any Cream of Wheat earrings. So the trip was a bust."

Dad opened his mouth to say something, but he stopped as two movers crossed from the dining room to the front door.

"Water break's over," said one of the men. "Now you'll need to tell us where to set down some bedroom furniture."

"Will do." They went outside, and Dad and I stood together at a window to watch the movers hoist Dad's bureau out of the truck.

While we watched, I told Dad about seeing Seth and his uncle.

"Two people from Sea Isle City," I said.

"That's a coincidence."

"And you know what else?" I asked, and I told him about how much Seth's uncle looked like Gary Carmichael.

"So you were scared," said Dad.

"Yeah, but it was for no reason. He didn't look much like Gary Carmichael from the front. A little, but his eyes are different and his nose isn't as long."

"At least it wasn't Carmichael."

"Was I glad about that!"

Chapter 22

As the summer wore on, Cassie and I hung around a lot together. She was easy to talk to and fun to be with. Sometimes we played soccer, and sometimes we watched butterflies dip and rise over the bushes in our backyards. Or sometimes we just sat and talked. I felt like I could say anything to her, and I wished I could tell her about the real reason Dad and I ended up being her neighbors.

I did tell her about Jellyfish one time when we were eating lunch on her patio. He seemed like a safe enough subject. I told her about how much I'd liked him and how little he'd noticed me.

"Finally I got his attention," I said, "and then we moved."

"Well," said Cassie, "as my grandmother would say, that's life."

"But Jellyfish was cool," I said. "And *so cute!*"

"Yeah." She lifted her soda can toward me. "Here's to the next cute Jellyfish and to the idea that he will be smart enough to notice you faster than his predecessor." We clinked cans. "Maybe Jellyfish's genes, anyway, aren't that great," she went on, "if he's as slow as all that. Maybe you didn't need jellyfish genes to combine with yours to make children. Think how many times you'd have had to ask one of your kids to take out the trash with those jellyfish genes getting in the way. Plus the whole transparent skin idea might really give you the creeps after a while."

I giggled. "Yeah." I clinked cans with her again. "To the new and improved Jellyfish, wherever you are."

"Anyway," said Cassie, and she was laughing too, "what do you need with a jellyfish when they've got sea bass out there and tarpons? And swordfishes. I've always wanted to date a swordfish."

"Seth doesn't look like a swordfish to me."

"I know. That's the problem. Not swordfish-like at all. I'm in such despair over it. *Oh! Look!*" as I giggled harder. "A female Eastern Tiger Swallowtail!"

That butterfly was so beautiful, I forgot to giggle. Entranced, we watched her in silence for about five minutes while she sat on a flower, her wings just opening and closing, opening and closing.

"Must be a lot of nectar in that flower for her," was Cassie's eventual comment.

"She makes this day perfect," I said.

And it was true. Peanut butter and jelly sandwiches. Ginger ale, blue sky, and a beautiful butterfly whose wings pulsed in the warm breeze. So dreamy and peaceful on Cassie's patio.

Ahhhhhh . . .

"Too bad you don't like to play basketball," Cassie said, "what with being so tall." Her voice sounded dreamy too.

"I think you need to have something besides height to be good at it. But I like to watch it, all right."

"I love basketball," said Cassie. "Once, my team almost made it to states. Boy, that three-pointer I almost got! If I'd gotten that, boy, we'd've gone for sure." She said it not like it was a disappointment but more like it was ice cream she'd gotten so close to tasting that she just knew how wonderful it would have been. "I'd never made a three-pointer, but I almost got that one." She smiled, her eyes focused on that memory. "Oh, boy. If I'd done that—"

I nodded, completely understanding. Well, not quite. Somehow her almost getting it seemed better than my success. How was that possible?

We did go to states. I didn't say it, but I wanted to. *And we won.* Was that a great game! I'd ridden high for about three weeks on that. It had been sooo cool. And Jellyfish—

I glanced at the hoop over Cassie's garage door, wishing for just one good play, just one good piece of footwork to get into place and *SHOT!* But then I returned my eyes to the butterfly. Still there. Still there.

"Isn't she amazing?" I asked.

Cassie nodded, and then we were just quiet. Quiet and watching the drama of the butterfly. Magical, even, in the soft August breezes. *This moment,* I felt, *will last forever.*

The butterfly lifted off the flower, and we watched as she flew around the side of the house.

"You're really a redhead." Cassie said it softly. Just said it. Not a question. A statement. A remark. Could have been *Those are cirrus clouds*, the way she said it. *You're really a redhead.*

Why'd she do that? Why'd she have to go and do that?

"How do you know?" Our voices were quiet, and we were both again looking at the flower where the butterfly had been. Anyone coming upon us would think we were talking about the flower or about maybe getting up for another ginger ale or who knows what. Certainly we couldn't have looked like one of us had just thrown a bomb at the other. Didn't she like me anymore?

"Your eyebrows. That red shows through the pencil sometimes. And you are tall."

"I don't know what being tall has to do with being a redhead." I took a nibble of my sandwich. "But it's true. I am a redhead." I glanced at Cassie's sharp green eyes, then glanced away. "So?" Nonchalant-sounding. But afraid. "No law against that." It did seem as though there was.

"Tall, redheaded, and athletic."

"I'm not athletic," I said. "Didn't you see me skid after that soccer ball this morning?" I looked down at my grass-stained knee. "As graceful as a gazelle."

She acted like she didn't hear me. "I saw those newspaper pictures of you on the basketball court. One of them showed a triangular birthmark when you hit the floor one time. It's on your back. I saw it today when you slid after the soccer ball, but I've known about you all along. You and your dad and that Broadway show. Both of you look like those pictures they had in the paper."

I put my sandwich down and stopped eating. Completely. Looked at Cassie and didn't say anything.

"Relax, Liza." She sounded so friendly and warm. Caring. "It's okay." Friendly? Warm? Caring? So?

"Never call me Liza."

"Fine. But look, Jennifer. I know. I'm not going to tell anybody, and I'll help you if you need anything. I'm your friend."

What to do, what to do? Deny it? Insist that I'm not Liza? But she knows!

Who else knew? Seth? Was his talk of Sea Isle City some kind of trap? Did he know Gary Carmichael after all? Maybe Carmichael was another uncle. He looked enough like the one I'd seen. Maybe Gary Carmichael had been in Sea Isle City for the family reunion. Maybe—

I stood up, not moving fast, not yet, but my heart sure was. Faster, faster, faster—*Go!*

"Wait! Wait!" Cassie caught up with me, circling a hand around my upper arm as I neared the property line.

I stopped and swung around, yanking free. "What?" Then I remembered Mom's hand in exactly the same place. *Mom!* I backed away, my palms up, stomach tightening. Fear. Fear was all around. "Please," I said. Was someone out there? Someone behind the hedges? Someone aiming? "Please."

I cringed for it, but there was no *Bang!* No *Bang!* and Cassie was still there, quietly unmoving against the gusty air that shook the branches and the bushes and my world. Her warm, unafraid eyes remained steady on mine. Why wasn't she afraid?

"I'm not going to tell," she repeated. "I just thought you'd like someone around who knew. Someone you can relax with and not have to worry every second that you might say the wrong thing."

No bang, no bang. Nobody attacking, nobody saving. Just Cassie and her soulful eyes.

Could I trust her? Did I dare? "You've known the whole time?"

"The whole time."

"And you didn't tell anyone? Not even Seth?"

"Not even Seth. And I won't. I promise."

I stepped around her. "I have to go."

"Wait." She turned and jogged sideways with me when I didn't stop. "Wait. Come on."

I slowed down. "What?"

"I want to give you something," she said. "Something that you have to promise never to look at. Then I'll be trusting *you.* It will go both ways."

"What is it? What could be as big a deal as my life and Dad's life?"

"It's my diary, and maybe it's not as big a deal as your lives, but it's something. You could ruin me with what's in it."

"I don't want it," I said. "I don't want to ruin anybody."

"Please?"

"I won't read it," I said, "but—"

"You won't read it, and I won't tell." Cassie paused. "Jennifer?"

"Yes?"

"I'm sorry about your mom. I've been wanting to say that all this time. I'm so sorry."

"Thank you." My eyes welled up, and for a few seconds I thought the tears would spill and I'd absolutely lose it. I blinked over them fast and swallowed hard. "It's good to have someone care."

It really was.

"Come with me. Just for a minute," said Cassie. "Please."

Still blinking back the tears, I reversed direction and followed Cassie into her house. We went up the stairs to her bedroom, and she pulled the diary out of a drawer for me. She fanned through the pages so I could look. "See?" she asked. "It really is my diary. See?" She stopped the pages sporadically as she spoke. "Here's the section about Seth when he broke up with me at Christmas." *Flip-flip-flip!* "And here's the section about when I flunked an English test because I had the flu." *Flip-flip!* "And here's the place where—"

"Never mind." I took the book and closed it to make her stop. "I don't need to know what's inside."

"If I rat on you," said Cassie, "you can do anything you want with this. Even call Seth and tell him what I wrote about him."

I can't call Seth if I'm dead. I pushed that thought away and said, "I won't do that." I tried to give back the book. "Keep it."

"No, no," she said. "You hold on to it. It's a sign of faith."

"It won't make any difference."

"That's okay. It makes me feel better somehow if you hold that sort of as collateral."

So I kept it. It felt heavy in my hand as we went back downstairs, and I looked for a place to leave it unnoticed—on a shelf or a table or the kitchen counter—before we left the house, but Cassie's eyes were on me the whole time, like she was afraid I was going to faint or run or disappear into thin air.

"I do feel better that you have that," she said. "It makes us more equal."

"I'll put it under my mattress," I told her. "If anything bad happens—"

"Nothing bad's going to happen," she said. "Only good things."

"Only good things," I repeated. "Like Eastern Tiger Swallowtails in backyard gardens."

"And eating together outside."

"And—and friendship."

"And friendship." Cassie gave me a hug. "I have to leave for the pool now," she said. "You're—you're not going to run or move or anything, are you, while I'm there?"

"I have to talk to Dad," I said.

She looked at me with those sea green eyes, and I looked back at her. Both looking, both asking. Was I seeing what I needed to see? Was she?

Then she nodded. "Do what you have to do," she said. "I know you're not in this alone. But I hope we can be friends whatever happens."

Then she left for the pool, and I went home, right away putting her diary under my mattress. Afterward I went downstairs and told Dad what Cassie knew. It was only fair. It wasn't only my life to be considered.

"Trusting her's a big risk," he said. "Do you believe her?"

"I believe her."

"It is a risk."

"I know. Maybe we shouldn't take the chance. Maybe we should leave."

I stood there watching Dad, almost seeing the gears turning inside his brain. He was my father. He had the right to make this decision without me. My trusting Cassie might not be enough to make a difference. Maybe, even if Cassie was trustworthy, it ought not to be. The stakes were so high.

Then Dad smiled at me. "We'll go with it," he said. "You could use a person to trust. You know her better than I do, but I think she's trustworthy too."

Chapter 23

Trusting Cassie made the summer so much better. Kicking soccer balls around, studying butterflies, shopping. Eating peanut butter sandwiches and reading together on her patio. Or ours. Drinking ginger ale. What would I have done without her?

"Hey, listen to this," she'd say, and read me something out of a magazine.

Or I'd say, "Listen to *this*," and share what funny thing I was reading.

Cool.

All those things and more I could do with her without always, always, always being on my guard. I was glad she knew.

One morning in early August we were laughing and shooting baskets when someone beyond Cassie emerged from the shadows around the side of her house.

Gary Carmichael. I knew it. He was the right height, anyway. Maybe I was wrong. Lots of people were six feet tall.

But then the bald head broke into the light. Blond fringe. How did he find me?

Cassie threw me the ball, but I was frozen, and it just bounced off my arm onto the blacktop.

"What's the matter?" asked Cassie, but then she saw him too. "Hey, Uncle Thaddeus!"

Oh. It wasn't Gary Carmichael. It was that mild-eyed guy from the mall, from Sea Isle City. Seth's uncle, wearing cutoffs and a stained Indians T-shirt. A hedge trimmer dangled heavily from his right hand.

I let out a huge breath and almost fell down with relief. Oh!

"Hey yourself," said the man, coming farther into the backyard. "I've come to trim the bushes." *Oh, yeah. He's a handyman.* But did he have to look so much like the guy with the knife? At least I'd had the sense to cover my red roots with my hat. But what if I hadn't? Would it have made any difference if the man had turned out to be from the Core? Why advertise, though? Anybody could talk to anybody who might know somebody who—

And why, oh why, was I playing basketball? I shouldn't have been playing basketball. No more basketball!

"It's about time," said Cassie. "Mom asks every day if you've been."

"Well, the next time she calls, you can tell her I was here."

Seth's uncle stopped and cocked his head at me. "You

look familiar." *Uh-oh.* "You're the girl behind the counter at that German bakery. Rosie's your name, right? I love your strudel."

Okay, he recognized me, but he put me in the wrong place. Good.

"Nope," I said. "I just moved in next door. I don't think I've been inside that bakery."

Cassie introduced us. "Jennifer Parker, Thaddeus Montgomery. Seth's uncle," she added, looking at me. "We saw him at the mall."

"Nice to meet you, Mr. Montgomery," I said. Cassie crossed her eyes at me and smiled. Okay, it was all right. She wasn't going to mention Sea Isle City.

"None of that 'mister' stuff," Seth's uncle said. "Everybody calls me Thaddeus. That's how history will remember me. Just Thaddeus."

I wasn't too sure I wanted to call him by his first name.

"*I* call him Uncle Thaddeus," said Cassie helpfully.

"Okay," said the man. "That works too." He held out his hand, and I shook it.

"What will history remember you for, Uncle Thaddeus?" I asked.

He released my hand. "Hedge trimming," he said. "I trim a beautiful hedge."

Then he went to work, Cassie went off to the pool, and I went home to dye my hair. Dad had been asking me about it every day.

"The red's really noticeable against the black," he'd said. "Those roots must be an inch long."

"I'll dye it," I kept telling him, "I will," but so far I hadn't, and what was the big deal if I could just wear the hat? Nobody could see through the hat, and I hated the way the dye smelled. I didn't want to put it on again. Plus I *liked* seeing the red hair as it came in little by little. It was *mine*, same as my Pennsylvania learner's permit was mine. Mine! Nobody was going to take it from me.

But that was all stupid, and after the second sort-of scare with Uncle Thaddeus, the stupidity burned.

I should die because of this? Why was I being so stupid?

What if Uncle Thaddeus had been the wrong person—and what if I hadn't been wearing my hat? What if it had fallen off while Cassie and I'd played? What if?

But Dad was in the shower when I entered the house, so instead of dyeing my hair—which I probably *still* could have done, because there *was* a kitchen sink—I took a Lisa Scottoline we'd borrowed from the library to read out on the front porch swing.

I'd go up and take care of my hair when I heard Dad come down the steps. Another ten minutes? It wouldn't matter. No one in the Core could see my red roots. No one in the Core knew where I was. No one in the Core probably even cared where I was. No one, no one, no one. So it wouldn't make any difference if I dyed my hair this minute or not.

I sat on the swing and opened my book.

Wait. Did I want one of the iPods? Scottoline and music and the soft summer air. Perfect. I'd set my watch for ten minutes in case the music blotted out Dad's footsteps.

But my iPod was in my bedroom, and I didn't feel like going all the way up there to get it. Jeff's was in the van, and— Oh, forget it! With an iPod on, I'd have to keep my hat on too, because it wouldn't be only Dad's footsteps I might miss with that music playing in my ear.

Not that anybody was coming. Nobody ever did.

But still . . .

I was hot and nobody was around, so—oh, what the heck!— I took off my hat. I'd hear anybody coming up the walk in time to put it back. Of course I would. That's what I told myself.

I knew better than to sit there hat-free. But I was so hot, I lied to myself. And believed the lie. Anyway, I'd hear . . .

Then I totally lost track of time and whatever else was going on around me. All I knew was the summer breeze and the story unfolding before my eyes.

It shouldn't have mattered. On any other day, it wouldn't have. Eventually I'd have gotten tired of reading and gone in and dyed my hair anyway, just later than I'd meant, and it wouldn't have mattered. Simple. Low key. No problem. Maybe had lunch afterward and not thought about it at all after that for the rest of my life. Any other day. But that one particular day, that one specific day that felt like any other—

Creak!

I dropped my book and jumped up, threw on my hat in

a rush, and shoved my hair under it, but it was too late. Mr. Barber, the man from the high school, finished climbing the wooden porch steps and stood before me. He'd seen. He'd seen.

"Wow!" Mr. Barber's eyes were bulging so far out of his head, it was amazing they didn't drop right down onto the floor and roll off into the garden.

Dad came out onto the porch then, and Mr. Barber stuck out his hand to be shaken and said why he was there.

That was the first thing he said, other than "Wow!" even though I was standing right there on the porch the whole time. I said "Hello," but Mr. Barber didn't answer. He acted like he didn't hear me, even though he sure could see me. He never said hello. Not to me. Nor good-bye, either, when he left.

"I always like to get a look at the home setting, uh-huh, uh-huh, for homeschoolers," he said to Dad, "and I happened to be nearby. Uh-huh, uh-huh. I hope you don't mind that I didn't call first. Uh-huh, uh-huh. I was down the street, and I thought I'd just swing over—"

Dad brushed away his words and invited him inside for a cup of coffee while they talked. I followed them inside and talked too, but I didn't think Mr. Barber processed anything either of us said. He could barely contain himself over his discovery. Twisting and contorting, he just could not sit still.

"Yessir," he said. "I just happened, uh-huh, uh-huh, to be in the neighborhood, and—"

Everyone in the country was wondering what had happened to Harold and Liza Wellington, but he *knew*. The man was practically jumping out of his skin, babbling and babbling, he was so obvious. In a minute he'd be writhing on the floor.

"We might have to shoot him and put him out of his misery," I told Dad. Mr. Barber didn't even hear me.

"All right, okay." Dad waved his hands to stop the flow of words. "You know who we are."

Mr. Barber admitted it, nodding and nodding. "Uh-huh, uh-huh. I saw the red hair. Uh-huh, uh-huh. And Liza's so tall."

"Call me Jennifer," I said, for all the good it did. I might have been speaking from Avon, Pennsylvania, which was where I wished I was.

"Uh-huh, uh-huh. How's the Broadway show going? Boy, it would be neat if you could come in and talk to one of the classes. The drama club goes to New York every spring break. They could see your musical. Hey, maybe you could—"

"I don't see how that's possible," interrupted Dad. "We're *hiding*."

"Oh-oh-oh! Well—um—"

"Forget you know us," my father said. "Don't tell *anybody*."

"Uh-huh, uh-huh, no problem. Uh-huh, uh-huh." But his eyes were on my hair, my eyebrows, and I don't think he really heard anything Dad said.

He just wanted to get out of our house and into his car so he could pull out his cell phone and call his wife or best friend—or

Gary Carmichael, for all I knew. *I know where Harold and Liza Wellington are. I know! I know!*

"Maybe," he went on, "after things are settled, uh-huh, uh-huh, you could come and talk."

"Sure," said Dad. "Maybe next year."

"Great!" Mr. Barber wrung Dad's hand. "I'll tell the drama coach," he said.

"No!" shouted Dad.

"Oh! I mean, uh-huh, uh-huh, when it's okay."

He left after that, half-running to his car, turning on the engine before he'd closed the driver side door. The car lurched into reverse and stalled on the street. Mr. Barber started the engine again, and then *screech!* off he went like he was two days late for his own wedding. It would have been funny if we hadn't known the why of it all.

Dad looked down at me with his eyebrows raised.

"How much time do you think we have?" I asked.

"Not much," he said. "Grab a couple of things, and we're history."

I sprinted up the stairs, pulled a few things out of their drawers, flung them onto the bed. Underwear, socks, shirts, shorts. What else? I glanced around the room. Hairbrush, deodorant, teddy bear—

A movement outside focused my eyes beyond the window.

Uncle Thaddeus was walking through our backyard. Why? Had Dad asked him to trim the bushes or something? But Dad didn't know Uncle Thaddeus.

I stared at Seth's uncle as he came closer. His eyes no longer looked mild, but searching and intense. Why? What was he looking for?

And why was he wearing a golf shirt instead of the Indians one? And why had his cutoffs become khakis?

And his temple—what was wrong with his temple?

His temple?

His *temple*?

No. No. Not Uncle Thaddeus.

No!

Chapter 24

I had a handful of Dad's shirt. "Looklooklooklook!" I jabbed at the kitchen window in front of us. "Looklooklook!"

No more words. Dad punched the garage door opener as I grabbed the keys off the kitchen table, and we charged out to the van. No time to waste handing the keys over, so I was driving! Dad took the seat beside me as the rearview mirror showed the rising of the garage door. Up, up, up—could it not move faster?

"Go!"

I stepped on the gas, and the van shot backward out of the garage. I turned the wheel too soon, driving over the grass, the curb, narrowly missing Cassie's mailbox and Uncle Thaddeus, who was trimming a bush beside it.

Reverse, reverse, reverse! I couldn't keep a straight course, but

I couldn't stop to change directions, either. No time for that. *Reverse, reverse, reverse!* I'd go where I had to go, but it was all going to be backward.

Bang! I hit a stop sign, and the van stalled.

"Aaa*ahh*!" I took it out of reverse, started the engine again. Forward!

The rearview mirror showed me Gary Carmichael racing for a green car parked a little ways down the street. A second man met him, speeding from the other side of our house. Two men? Two green doors opened, two green doors closed, and Gary Carmichael's car pulled away from the curb. Two men. Only two. At least in the green car. Were there other cars?

"Faster," hollered Dad. "Faster!"

We went through stop signs and ran yellow lights. Yellow into red. Some red. We just didn't stop. Neither did the green car.

Smash! The driver side mirror flew apart.

"Get down! Get down!"

Dad dropped to the floor between the seats.

Bang! Something else shattered. I didn't know what, but I kept driving.

Screech!

Honk, honk, hooooonk!

Bang!

I kept my right foot all the way down to the floor, and I held my breath. Would we live another minute? Another second?

Cars sped toward us as we approached an intersection, but

there was a small gap. Not moving my foot, I fishtailed a left. *Screeeech!*

Hoooonk!

The rear of the van pulled to the right, then to the left while I fought with the steering wheel. Finally I straightened out the vehicle. Where could I go? The green car was no longer behind us, but Gary Carmichael had seen where we went. How soon would traffic allow him and his buddy to follow us? I glanced back and saw a steady line of traffic crossing the intersection. But that wouldn't last. Not knowing what else to do, I kept on, foot on the floor, foot on the floor.

Trees to the right, trees to the left! No place to go! Gary Carmichael would catch us! Trees to the right, to the left! *Come on, come on!*

Green and shadows and tree trunks all flashed by. No time to look, no time to figure anything out, but I had to figure something out.

Then a spot.

I didn't think. I just turned. Barely braking, I fishtailed us toward a barely visible path, praying it really was a path, praying we wouldn't hit a tree, praying the fishtail wouldn't turn us over as we jumped the curb.

Bump, bump, bump, bump!

We kept going. I couldn't see any boulders, but it sure felt like we were bouncing over them.

Bump, bump, bump, bump! Then a wide oak showed up in front of us, and I hit the brakes. We slid into it and jolted to a stop.

Whew! Were we okay? The rearview mirror showed no car behind us. And we'd turned somehow, so I couldn't see as far as the opening to the road.

"I think we lost them, Dad." I was out of breath. "Are you all right?"

"Scared to death," he answered. He pulled himself up onto the passenger seat and looked behind. "You're amazing."

I removed my hands from the steering wheel. They were shaking. Dad took them and held them between his.

"We have to get out of the van," he said. "We're sitting ducks if they see it."

Carefully, as quietly as we could, we left the open-doored vehicle and the path, and we entered the woods.

"Do you have a phone?" I whispered.

"No. You?"

"No."

We stood there for a long time. Where should we have gone? Anywhere could have led us to Gary Carmichael.

Shadows shifted and lengthened, and still we stood.

I touched Dad on the arm. "What do you think?" I barely breathed out the words.

"Let's walk back to the road before we return to the van," he murmured. "Make sure there's nobody waiting for us when we back out."

I nodded.

"Be ready to run," he added.

We crept back alongside the path, staying behind the trees,

looking everywhere, over our shoulders, up in the branches, through the woods, for a sign that Gary Carmichael and his buddy were near.

The hair all over my head stood on end. Something brushed my arm, and I ran, crashing through the underbrush. Oh. Only a leaf. Only. I slowed down and walked carefully again, hoping my sudden dash hadn't been heard. I looked at Dad.

"It's okay," he mouthed.

Finally, still half-hidden, we reached a place where we could look out at the street. Nothing much to see. No parked cars anywhere. The air was still, and the passing motorists drove like everything was ordinary. No fishtailing. No horns blowing. No screeching of tires. Ordinary. How could everything be so ordinary?

"Okay," whispered Dad, and we started back to the van. I hoped it would start. With all the boulder-hopping and the jolting stop, maybe I'd wrecked something. But there weren't any boulders that I saw. Just tree roots and fallen branches. And maybe hitting the tree wouldn't mean anything.

Then—Gary Carmichael. Right there.

I pulled on Dad's arm to stop him. Gary Carmichael was facing the other way and didn't see us, but I saw the lump on his temple. No maybe-Carmichaels here. Only the real kind. Where was the other guy?

Dad pointed up. *Climb!* But what would he do? I made a face that asked that, but he just pointed up. I nodded, but mouthed to him, pointing, "Go." So if I made noise climbing, Gary Carmichael wouldn't see Dad right away, and he'd have a head start. He'd have a head start and he'd get away—he'd get away and find help.

Dad disappeared quietly into the thickness, and I climbed. Every time I reached another branch, I looked to see if Gary Carmichael had moved.

He hadn't.

He hadn't.

He hadn't.

"Got him!" My head snapped toward the street at the shout. There in a clearing was Dad, struggling with Carmichael's buddy. Two other men turned up, and Dad stopped fighting. And then Gary Carmichael was with them. No way could Dad get away. What would happen next? What could I do?

"Where is she?" Carmichael's words cracked the summer air. "Where's your girl? Where's your girl?" *Whack!* A blow to Dad's weak shoulder. The men knew. Coffee, perfect pitch, *eyes*, and *SHOULDER!* They knew. And all of them had to know that I was watching and that I would come down to make them stop. I WOULD!

Carmichael hit Dad again.

DON'T YOU DARE!

But before I could make more than a move downward, Dad bellowed, "NO, LIZAAAA!"

This time when Carmichael took a swing, Dad slumped to the ground. "That's all right," said one of the others, nudging him with his foot. "He'll come to in a minute, and I'll hit him again. He'll tell us where she is."

I looked around. A pair of girls was just entering the path from the street. One was picking up litter and putting it into a big trash bag. The other had a cell phone to her ear.

I didn't think about it. I climbed down fast, and took the path toward them. Silent, silent, but fast. Could this work? Could it?

I met the girls, both about twelve years old, not far from where the men stood, and I smiled at them. I couldn't see the men, and I hoped they couldn't see me, but I knew they were in there.

I picked up some pretend litter—a couple of leaves and a twig—I didn't see any of the real stuff—and I placed it in the bag.

The girls smiled at me.

Then—*Yes!*—the one with the phone got a startled *I know you* look. "Mom, guess what?"

I put a finger over my lips. "Quietly." The word came with almost no sound. I hoped the men hadn't heard her, but maybe it wouldn't matter. If I moved fast enough.

The other girl pulled a phone out of her own pocket and gestured. "Photo?" she mouthed.

I didn't answer, just left the path. I turned, and the girls were following me, Picture-girl getting me in her sights, Mom-girl whispering into her phone. I put my finger to my mouth again, and they nodded conspiratorially, still following, following, but not too close.

Then it was just me emerging toward the men circled

around Dad, just me becoming visible to them. Would this work? Would it? I broke a twig with my foot—*snap*—and they saw me.

"*AAAAAAAAAGGHHH!*" I let loose. "*AAAAAAAAAGGGHHH!*"

"Mom!" *FLASH!* "Call the police!"

The men scattered, so—*FLASH!*—the second picture was blurred. So was the first one, but no one knew that. The men— they were just gone.

Chapter 25

Dad and I were back in Avon, and there were balloons everywhere decorating our backyard for the big Labor Day barbecue we had every year. Jellyfish had his arm around me, and oh-oh-oh, was that wonderful! Behind him, a big cake decorated with pink and white frosting shouted WELCOME HOME! in pink letters.

"Now," he said, "how about that movie?"

I could hardly talk, I was so happy.

It was all a mistake. How could we have thought otherwise?

It was all a mistake. Wasn't that great? No one had shot Mom. The bang had been a backfire, and the red on her shirt, that had been from the sticker bushes. She was still alive, even though they'd pronounced her dead. Sometimes that happens. You've seen it on TV. And she'd woken up in the morgue, and they hadn't been able to find us because we'd been running.

It was all a mistake, and Dad and I got to go home again, back to our old house with Mrs. Pomeroy and the Carters and Mr. Solomon still living right nearby. And Mom standing on our front steps with her arms open wide.

The whole neighborhood came to the party. Jackie and Jellyfish, and even Ms. Mallory, my principal. I loved everybody, and it was so great to see everyone. Even Hanna and Cassie and Seth and Uncle Thaddeus were there. I thought I would just about die, I was so happy. No more hiding, no more hiding, no more—

That was what I wanted. That was what I really wanted. And if you like happy endings, this is where you should stop, where it all comes together beautifully and my existence returns to what it was.

But my life turned out to be more ragged than that.

We had a sort of happy ending, Dad and I. We lived through it all. At least we have so far, and that's pretty happy. You can't have a future if you're dead, so we have futures.

Dad's shoulder is better than it has been since that car accident way back in his twenties. That's what the surgery did, the surgery Dad had to have after the beating Carmichael and his buddies gave him. That part I don't want to think about. But they hurt him bad. At least now it's better.

And we sneaked into his show. It wasn't anywhere near

opening night, and nobody knew we were coming. It was good. Almost sold out. Good thing for the "almost" part, or we wouldn't have gotten in.

"It was a risk," Dad said later over ice cream at a place halfway to nowhere. "Maybe we won't do that again."

"I'm glad we went," I said. "It looks like they're making you some bucks too. Anyway, anybody looking for us there gave up months ago." Maybe.

What we think happened back in the underpass is this: I really did see Robert Bramwell—who is now under indictment on drug and money laundering charges—there when members of the Core killed Charles McVoy before he could turn state's evidence on them. Before anybody could figure out Bramwell's connection to the Core and where so much of his money came from. The Core gathered in the underpass to kill McVoy, and then I—acting just like a regular person—showed up and scrambled their strategy.

Except I didn't know. If they had done nothing after I'd run away from them, if they hadn't aimed their guns and had just let me go home with my mother, nobody would have ever known what had really happened in that tunnel. Even me.

Thank goodness for those girls picking up litter. Without them on the spot, we'd have been dead. And thank goodness for Mr. Barber. He'd put us on the alert even if he had nothing to do with the Core. If Dad hadn't taken a shower that afternoon, if I'd dyed my hair instead of reading on the porch, if Mr. Barber hadn't shown up at our house and acted so strangely right then—all those details—if they hadn't happened the way they had—well, it would have ended right there.

We did figure out how the Core found us in Ohio. A device that someone had planted in Jeff's iPod pinpointed us. Who, we didn't know, maybe Jeff. But if so, maybe it didn't transmit so well in Kansas. Or it just took the Core a while to decide to follow us there. Maybe all the publicity and the reward pushed them to go after us faster than they might have. Or maybe one of them planted the bug in Kansas once we'd fled.

We can only guess.

But we're pretty sure the Core had no more idea where we were after we left Kansas than the rest of the world, not until Dad picked the iPod up at the RadioShack the day before Gary Carmichael walked through our backyard.

Dad and I—we're okay. We're on our own since the hospital, telling nobody, not even the FBI, where we are. Homeschooling? Whatever. Survival is what's important. That's been the name of the game all along.

I can't tell you where we are, but it probably wouldn't matter. We might not be here tomorrow or next week or next month. Because eventually, something happens—we recognize somebody or somebody gets a funny look in his eye, and we go!

Someday, somewhere, I hope we'll stay. School, friends, basketball, college . . . all that, some day.

In the meantime, love to everybody who loves us. Hope to see you again sometime.

Susan Shaw is the author of *One of the Survivors*, about which Jerry Spinelli said, "Susan Shaw peels the layers away until nothing is left but the seed—and it is both terrible and wonderful." Susan also wrote *Black-eyed Suzie*; *Safe*, an ALA Top Ten Quick Pick for Reluctant Young Adult Readers and a Carolyn W. Field Honor Book; and *The Boy from the Basement*, a Junior Library Guild Selection and a New York Public Library Book for the Teen Age. She lives in Wayne, Pennsylvania, and you can visit her online at SusanShaw.org.